# THE TF-77 TRILOGY

## BOOKS 1-3

## CHASE AUSTIN

YOUR FREE BOOK

**Do not forget to download your FREE COPY of WICKED STORM.**

**Click the link - www.thechaseaustin.com**

# FORCE RECRUIT

## TASK FORCE THRILLER #1

# ABOUT FORCE RECRUIT

*From the Author of the breakthrough Sam Wick Rapid Thriller Series, a breathtaking, page-turning novel about a disgraced female detective's fight for redemption. And survival...*

*Karen Jones was a promising young police detective when she got embroiled in a controversial trial for the murder of a homicide suspect. Traumatized, betrayed, and publicly vilified, Karen could only watch as her career rapidly descended towards its premature end. Her boss--a decorated officer--offered his help to get her out of this mess but it came with a huge cost.*

*Karen wanted to be in the force to make a difference but now she had to decide between selling her soul or pursuing this dream she had woven together with her father. The clock is ticking and Karen had to choose her options very fast.*

# CHAPTER 1

NEW JERSEY, USA

The smell of burlap overwhelmed Karen. She attempted to untangle herself, but the nylon rope was stiff around her body, keeping her fastened to the wooden chair. As her senses gradually returned to normal, she began to feel every bone in her body aching. She didn't know if her eyes were open or not; the darkness in the burlap was frightening. She had no idea where she was, why she was there and how she got there?

Her situation seemed hopeless, but suddenly her survival instincts began to kick in to keep her from sinking. She felt an unknown anger swelling within her; anger about everything that had happened to her in the last few weeks. How she had been used and abused by the powerful and everything that had taken her towards destruction. Everyone has a breaking point, and this was probably hers. She felt her ears getting warmer, her teeth clenching, her nostrils flaring, her fists tightening. In that moment of heat, she made a decision—she would not succumb to this. She will not die here. Not before finding out who did this to her, and for that she had to conserve her energy. She took a deep breath to calm her nerves, but the stench of the sack made her dizzy again.

She tried to remember the last place she had been before being here.

And then she recollected. She recalled the dark corridors of the Pelican motel. She remembered strutting away from the building in a hurry.

What time did that happen? She remembered checking her cell phone—it had been somewhere around midnight. The whole department was busy celebrating pre-Christmas Eve at Gilly's—one of the best barbeque bars of the locality—but she wasn't there. She was in Pelican—a shady motel—doing something that she shouldn't be doing. And when she had just managed to get out of there, she had woken up here. What had really happened?

She was awake but remained frozen in the same posture. She didn't know who was watching her and what they would do if they saw her coming back to senses. She had to figure out things before doing anything else.

Gradually, she started to connect the dots. The haze started to thin. The first thing that became clear to her was that the people behind this either didn't know who she was or didn't care about what she did for a living. Kidnapping a detective wasn't a joke. The chances were high that the people behind her abduction knew of her identity.

So the question was why—why had they still done it?

Abducting her made no sense. She didn't fit the profile. She wasn't loaded. Suspended from work, she wasn't a threat to anyone except, maybe, herself. She was a nobody and what she had done before being kidnaped had the upshots of her being staying a nobody all her life. There weren't many loose threads to connect but still she racked her brain. So much so that she forgot that she was still tied to a chair and should be panicking.

She knew no one was coming to save her. Even if it wasn't for the party, they weren't going to come looking for her. She was suspended from the department because of the ongoing court case and had not spoken to anyone since she visited the station last, a few weeks ago.

She knew that they considered her a black mark on the department's ledger, especially for her court case. She had heard this quite a few times behind her back and, occasionally, to her face. It was, in a way, better that the kidnappers would kill her on realizing no one would look for her. It was a strange situation; the kidnappers must know about the court case. It was the headline of every city newspaper from the day it started. And if they knew about that, then they couldn't have missed the fact that she was under suspension. Did they mistake her for someone else?

Perhaps, but now what? Would they kill her or give her a safe passage out?

She didn't know how much time she had spent since waking up, but she didn't care about things not in her control. All she could do now was think about her options and she kept at it, despite most scenarios ending nowhere. Deep down, she wanted her humiliation to end. She was just twenty-six, yet in a strange way the fact that someone considered her worth killing was oddly comforting.

As her mind started to calm, her ears picked up music coming from an obviously shitty radio. Taylor Swift's "Starlight" was playing. Hearing the lyrics, something inside her stirred, and she squirmed with pain and guilt. Outwardly, though, she remained frozen. A plethora of contradictory emotions rose and ebbed within her in a very short span of time. She wanted to cry but couldn't. She wanted to yell, but couldn't. She shut her eyes tight and then, as if from the depths of despair, her father's words rose to overpower her vacillation. "You are my star and you will always be." His voice echoed in her ears.

Though sweating and dehydrated, her thoughts now started to move towards hope, calm as the morning sun. Her eyes had started to burn, but something inside her was solidifying. She would not be a victim. She would not bow down. She would fight until her last breath.

But she had to wait for the right time. She had already tested the ropes around her. They were tied in a way that the more you struggled, the more they clawed into your skin. It was best to save her strength. She would need it; she would need her focus. What awaited her on the other side of the sack was unknown. The best thing she could do was to be ready. Her head kept lolling as if in sleep, her chin touching the upper part of her chest. Her body was fluid, like a napping cat, but her mind was alert.

# CHAPTER 2

The place was filled with the peculiar mix of the dominant and the fringe of the city: judges, lawyers, business executives, and law enforcement personnel, together with the mentally ill, the homeless, felons and ex-felons, paralegals and illegals. Christmas was approaching and holiday decorations could be seen on the lamp-posts outside and decking nearby buildings. In front of the federal building stood a 15-foot tall Christmas tree, its better days far behind it.

On the steps of the district court plaza, two cameramen were setting up their tripods, video cameras and a microphone tree. No cameras were allowed in the federal court. Detective Karen Jones, in her mid-twenties, tough and wounded, stood by the statue of the blindfolded Lady Justice, smoking.

.   .   .

Her eyes tracked an attractive blonde as she hurried up the steps and through the heavy glass doors. She shot the cigarette butt into a trashcan and followed her in.

# CHAPTER 3

In the courtroom, Karen sat at one of the tables next to Assistant City Attorney Roger Wilson. The blonde she had followed into the courthouse sat at the other table: Pamela Rodriguez, mid-thirties, killer eyes, killer legs, and exceptionally good at what she did. Next to her was Luis Sanchez and his wife.

A full jury was seated in the box. In the public gallery, several reporters, including newspapers like the New York Times and a sketch artist were poised to capture the personalities of the case. Judge Benjamin Anderson, fifties, northern and courtly, entered from the chambers and took the bench.

"All rise. The United States District Court for the District of New Jersey, Judge Benjamin Anderson presiding, is now in session. All persons having business before the court draw near and you shall be heard. Be seated." The bailiff shouted.

.   .   .

Everyone settled, including the judge.

Anderson began, "In the matter of Sanchez versus Jones, are we ready for opening statements?"

"Yes, Your Honor, the plaintiffs are ready to proceed." Ms. Rodriguez rose and then sat down.

Wilson rose, all 300 pounds of him. "Your Honor, the defense is ready." The judge looked at detective Karen Jones, sitting beside Wilson—her defence attorney.

"Very well then," Anderson said. He turned his attention to the jury. "Ladies and gentlemen, thank you for being on time this morning. We will begin our trial today with opening statements from the attorneys for both sides. These statements are not to be construed as anything like actual evidence. The attorneys, being attorneys, may make some lofty allegations, but just because they say it, doesn't make it true."

Polite smiles and chuckles from the jury vibrated through the room.

Anderson continued, "It will be up to you to decide if what the lawyers allege in these statements is, in fact, proven during this trial. The plaintiffs always go first. Ms. Rodriguez, you have the floor." He ended with a glance at Luis Sanchez and his wife.

· · ·

Rodriguez stood and moved to a lectern that stood off the corner of the jury box. She smiled and began making eye contact with each of the jurors in turn. "The judge is right when he tells you that the statement I'm about to make is only a blue-print, a road map, if you will, of the case I will present on behalf of my clients, Luis Sanchez and his wife, Elena Sanchez. I would like to take you down that road a piece..." She shot a quick glance in Anderson's direction, to see if that bit of folksy landed. Karen glanced at Wilson, who rolled his eyes at Rodriguez's homespun approach.

"This is not a criminal case. You may believe that what happened to my clients' son was criminal but, in this courtroom, we are trying a civil matter. It involves the fatal shooting of a man named Alejandro Sanchez, a loving son and an upright citizen." She glanced at Luis and Elena, sitting tearfully at the plaintiff's table, "Most of all, this case is about a police officer who wasn't satisfied with her job and the vast powers that come with it. She also wanted your job, ladies and gentlemen of the jury. And Judge Anderson's job. In fact, she wanted the state of New Jersey's job, the job of administering verdicts and sentences, and especially, carrying out executions. She wanted it all. This case is about that officer, Detective Karen Jones, sitting at the defendant's table." As she turned to look at her, all eyes traveled to Karen.

Rodriguez looked at each juror and then politely thanked everyone before going back to her seat. Karen tracked Rodriguez back to her table and caught the wife, Elena, staring daggers at her. Unnerved, she turned away like a guilty person.

.   .   .

"We will take a brief recess before we hear from Mr. Wilson," Anderson said.

"All rise." The bailiff spoke again. As Anderson stood, everyone else followed.

* * *

Outside the courthouse, a homeless man was rooting in the ash-can for left-over butts, mumbling to himself, as Karen smoked by the statue, watching the TV reporters tape a standup report on Rodriguez's opening. Her words drifted across the plaza.

"... The wrongful death civil suit of the homicide detective Karen Jones opened today in federal court in New Jersey. Detective Jones is being sued by the family of Alejandro Sanchez, a man detective Jones believed to be a runway criminal wanted in five cases. The family contends that Alejandro was not the wanted man, and that he was unarmed the night detective Jones shot and killed him. Although detective Jones was cleared by the NJPD, questions remain about exactly what happened that night..."

"Christ's sake," Karen muttered under her breath. She looked over as the homeless man abruptly stopped mumbling, looked up at someone approaching and dashed away. Karen turned; it was Rodriguez, lighting a smoke of her own.

"You scared him off," Karen said.

. . .

"He knows me. He used to be a lawyer. He's embarrassed for me to see him like he is now."

"What happened to him?"

"Long story. Ask Wilson. Maybe he'll tell you."

"You hate Wilson?" Karen asked.

"What's there to like? Wilson works for the city; He doesn't have to know how to win. He just has to know how to settle. At least I know what it's like to win. Speaking of which, can I ask you something—just you and me here?" Rodriguez looked at Karen for the first time since she was standing with her. Karen nodded. "Why didn't the city settle this case? It could've all gone away for a couple hundred grand. They do it every week."

"I wouldn't let them. I told them I'd go out and get my own lawyer if they tried to settle." Karen looked over to the TV reporter, who was interviewing a nameless citizen. "And raise a shit storm with the media." she added.

"That jury gets two weeks of watching the couple crying their eyes out every day. They'll make that two hundred grand a drop in the bucket." Rodriguez paused, but Karen only shrugged. "You do know that if they award punitive damages, the city doesn't cover you, right? That comes out of your pocket. You have that kind of money squirreled away, detective? You crooked and brutal?"

Karen took a long drag, exhaled, and looked right at her. "Your client's son was a rapist and a murderer."

"Not proved."

"They had to know, but they looked the other way. Turned a blind eye."

"I'd like to see you prove that, too. I'd like to see you prove anything. Other than the one incontestable fact of this case— that you killed Alejandro Sanchez."

"And I'd do it again."

"I know you would, detective. I know you would. That's why we're here. To stop you from doing it again to someone else. I'm on. Stick around. You might learn something." Rodriguez stubbed out her cigarette before heading towards the cameras. Karen watched her go.

* * *

Wilson's opening was underway. "... the law gives a police officer the right to use deadly force if he believes he is in danger."

. . .

17

In the Courtroom Artist's sketch of Wilson at the lectern, he showed him as a fat belly up man. Karen was sitting at the defence table, staring straight ahead, unable to look at her lawyer, who she and everyone else knew was a second-tier talent, compared to Rodriguez. "Which is what Detective Karen Jones believed. That her life was in danger. A dark rainy night, an ill-lit street, a crime-ridden neighborhood, a dedicated detective in hot pursuit of a serial killer." Wilson continued.

"Objection. An unproven characterization, your honor." Rodriguez was up on her feet.

"Which is exactly what this trial is for, Ms. Rodriguez," Anderson said calmly. "I did not allow Mr. Wilson to interrupt your opening, which, I might add, was replete with unproven characterizations of Detective Karen Jones."

"Yes, your honor. I apologize." Rodriguez sat swiftly. Wilson, although a little thrown by the interruption, continued. "A police officer in threatening, possibly dangerous circumstances, trying to apprehend a suspect, is allowed, under the law, to use deadly force when he believes his own life is in jeopardy. The facts of this case will show that Mr. Sanchez ignored Detective Karen Jones's repeated commands to stop moving and put up his hands. He ignored repeated commands to keep his hands in plain sight. Let me quote Sun Tzu in The Art of War. When Detective Karen Jones encountered Sanchez on that dark, rainy street three years ago, she entered what Sun Tzu called the Dying Ground. At that point, Detective Karen Jones had to fight or perish, shoot or be shot. To second guess her actions now are impossible—and unfair. We weren't there. We didn't have to make that split second, life-or-death decision. Detective Jones reacted as she should have—just as all her training and experience taught her to—with deadly force. Mr. Sanchez had only himself to blame. His death was a result of the choices he made that night. Detective Karen Jones acted properly, under the color of law..." He paused at the end of his statement and thanked everyone.

Wilson shuffled over to his place and sat down. Karen glanced at the jury. They seem unmoved, blasé. Judge Anderson shuffled papers. He seemed to have lost interest halfway during Wilson's statement. "Ladies and gentlemen, I think that's enough for today. We are going to take tomorrow off, to separate opening statements from the start of the plaintiff's case." he announced. The courtroom started to stir, relieved. Anderson continued. "Please remember the court's admonishment to avoid reading or listening or watching any media reports on this trial. I wish you all a good weekend. Thank you all very much."

"All rise."

The judge left the bench, and the jury shuffled through the rear door to the assembly room. The media exited first. Rodriguez and the Sanchez family were in tow. Wilson leaned back. "What do you think?"

Karen pushed her chair back and got up. Without saying anything, she left Wilson in a pool of his own flop sweat. She knew how this case would pan out with Wilson on her side.

# CHAPTER 4

In the precinct, Karen walked past a couple of custodies cuffed to a bench. She stepped through the back door of the detective bureau. Being a late afternoon on Friday, the bullpen was half empty. Her desk was at the far-away corner from the entrance assigned to the rookies.

She wasn't a rookie, yet she sat there. But it wasn't always so. A top graduate from the academy, she had had a promising start at a small-town station under the tutelage of the town Sheriff. Each case she solved led to her meteoric rise in the town and, eventually, it reached the people who could elevate her to the heights she deserved.

She had shifted her base to the New Jersey police department almost a year ago, with big dreams in her eyes.

What she didn't know was that it wouldn't be the criminals, but the department's internal politics and her instincts—which had earlier led her to the right path—that would be her biggest impediments. After a year-and-a-half of sub-par performance, she was still measured like a newbie in the precinct along with her partner, who was inept at best because of his inability to capture the basics of a fact. She hated her partner, and she knew that the feeling was mutual. And then, during one operation, she accidentally shot Alejandro Sanchez, allegedly involved in a rape case and multiple homicide cases. The department had promised to back her, but once the case moved to the court, the tables turned quickly. The department's patience seemed to wear thin and the people who had backed her earlier were now slowly turning against her.

At times, she thought of running away.

This too shall pass, she thought and stayed.

But she had no idea that this was just the beginning. The worst was yet to come.

# CHAPTER 5

Karen walked to her desk in the bullpen amidst the usual clutter: file cabinets, counters, desks, and every flat surface awash with files and paperwork.

Her desk was neat and orderly, stacked on both sides with files. The surface was glass-topped and beneath the glass were several photos of different men and women, and a few children —victims in cases she was still working. There was a coffee mug full of pens. On the wall next to the desk was a bulletin board cluttered with various reports and messages. A yellowed printout in large block letters pinned in a corner: Success comes to those who knock on doors. Partially hidden was an old photo of her father and her old team. Usually, a smile came to her face looking at those, but not today. The other corner was some-what plain looking.

She started looking through a stack of phone messages.

. . .

"Jones." Someone called her name. She raised her head and looked toward the lieutenant's office on the other side of the squad room. Lt. Robert Wade, 45, was standing in the doorway, signaling her over. The few other officers smirked at the call.

Karen walked over, consciously avoiding their faces.

Wade seemed all business while he closed the door. His desk had a sign with his name on it and photos of his family. He was a proud family guy and a devout Christian. Although he said enough times that he believed in his people and their integrity, Karen knew that when the shove comes to push, for him the color of the law was thicker than human blood. She ignored everything else in the room. She had seen this enough times.

"What're you doing here, Jones?"

"We're recessed for the weekend. I thought I'd come by to check my messages, you know?"

"No, I don't know. You're off the rotation and, technically, on inactive status until there's a verdict. So, go home. Now."

"I was just about to leave." Karen turned to leave the room.

"How'd opening statements go?" Wade asked in a different tone, and Karen had to stop.

. . .

"Ordinary."

"How's Wilson doing?"

"About what you'd expect. She's the majors. He's double-A, maybe, on his best day. And he'll never hit a big-league curveball even to save his life."

"Karen, the department is feeling a lot of heat because of this case. Till now, I'm the one standing between you and your downfall. Just don't fuck this up."

"I'm not trying to."

"Good, you can go. Also, Superintendent Hudson has asked for you. He wanted to see if he can help us in any way, but he wants to hear your version before making up his mind. This could be the shot that we need to get you and the department out of this mess. Call his assistant, Samara, and get an appointment."

"Okay."

"Jones, I'm not getting the feeling that you're taking all this seriously. If that's the case then let me know, I have a hundred other places to divert my attention."

.　.　.

"Lieutenant, I'm committed to clear my name." Karen forced the words out of her mouth.

"Good." Wade dug his head in thick files. Karen left without saying anything further.

# CHAPTER 6

Six days ago

Karen was waiting in the lobby outside Superintendent Hudson's office. At 63, Hudson was America's most respected police chief. This reflected, in part, Hudson's breadth of experience: 29 years working his way up the chain of command in Chicago, eight years as police chief in Washington, D.C., and eight years at the helm in New Jersey.

Equally important was his passion for the profession and his care for his officers. In his office, five officer portraits occupied a position of prominence on the wall behind his desk. They were the officers who had been killed on the job since he became superintendent. Hudson could recite the details of every single killing with encyclopedic precision—date, time, circumstances, survivors. There were other reasons behind the respect that Hudson commanded. His word was good. He was savvy. There was just a direct honesty about him. It also helped that he had a good sense of humor.

It was not surprising that, last year, the U.S. President tapped Hudson to take on the current challenges of policing by co-chairing, along with Robinson, his Task Force on 21st Century Policing. By accepting the position and helping craft a blueprint for change, Hudson had put an emphatic exclamation point on his career and had taken a big chance. The task force's final report, issued in May, included ideas that challenged some of his profession's most cherished tenets. In particular, it called for moving oversight of alleged police wrongdoing out of police departments and even local prosecutors' offices, vesting it in outside agencies or task forces instead. Hudson has also promoted a promising yet unproven approach known as procedural fairness to strengthen police-community relations. He had endorsed radical changes to how police departments operate internally and questioned their current focus on intelli-gence gathering.

These suggestions had made even the non-believers believe in him. Karen had been one of them.

"He will see you now." Samara, Hudson's personal assistant, nodded her head.

Karen stood up and took some time to straighten her uniform. She was a little overwhelmed by the opportunity to meet the chief for the first time, particularly as that man was Hudson. She was suspended, but felt it important to be in her uniform when meeting the most powerful man in the state police. Still trying hard to overcome her feelings of inferiority, the stare from Samara made her walk towards the door in a hurry.

In the office, Hudson was sitting at his desk, reading a thick file. But that was not the first thing that Karen had noticed. The first thing was the five officer portraits hanging on the wall behind Hudson's desk, whom she had seen only in photos.

"Detective Jones, please sit down," Hudson spoke without looking up from the file.

"Thank you, Sir," Karen said awkwardly and sat down.

"Just give me a moment to finish this. If you would like to have something like coffee, you can use the coffee maker there." He said politely, but still looking at the file.

"Thank you, Sir. I'm good."

"I've been told that this is an exquisite machine, but I've never come around to using it," Hudson raised his eyes from the file to Karen, a smile playing on his lips. "I still call Samara to brew me a cup whenever I need one. At least if you use it then you can share your unbiased views on whether the machine company's claims are correct, or if it is just a marketing gimmick."

· · ·

Karen smiled in response and rose to make coffee.

"Make one for me too, if you don't mind. These pages are mind-numbing." Hudson said from behind.

"Sure Sir."

"I prefer it if people call me Hudson. That way I don't feel that I'm too old for this job."

Karen had heard about his sense of humor and his preference to be on a first name basis with his colleagues, but she didn't know how much of it was true.

"Yes, sir. I mean, Hudson." They both looked at each other, and then Hudson turned back to his file. For the next few minutes, the machine's whirring and whizzing was the only thing breaking the silence of the office.

And then a knock on the door broke Karen's concentration. It was Samara, Hudson's personal assistant.

"Yes, Samara?" Hudson looked at her with indifference.

"I'm leaving for the day."

.   .   .

"For the doctor's appointment?"

"Yes," Samara said.

"Okay, see you tomorrow." Hudson turned back to his files.

Samara gave a blank stare to Karen, who stood near the coffee machine. The stare remained a second longer than necessary and then she slowly closed the door behind her. It was her first meeting with Samara, but Karen was already finding her too weird to ever meet again. The machine made a wheezing sound while emanating steam and Karen's train of thought was interrupted.

"I think the coffee is ready, and so are we," Hudson spoke while slowly rising from his seat.

The sentence surprised Karen, who suddenly found herself conscious. At the outset, she wasn't ready for a cup of coffee with the boss of all her bosses. She had to quickly calm herself.

"Sugar?" she asked.

"At my age, I have to say no." Hudson smiled again.

.   .   .

Karen found some of her lost confidence in Hudson's charming demeanor. She took him his cup. Hudson took it without touching Karen's hand.

"Where do you want us to sit?" he asked.

Karen looked around the room. There was a couch set at the right side of the door, along with a large mahogany table. It was a very simple arrangement, but the couch seemed unique. A piece of fine craftsmanship which, unfortunately, also made it seem incongruent with the rest of the office décor.

"I got this from a Tibetan shop. Very fine artistry. One of my favorite possessions."

Karen couldn't agree more. She had seen nothing like it before.

"We can sit there, no need to stare at it while our coffee is getting colder," Hudson said, and Karen found herself slightly embarrassed. She was, indeed, staring at the couch for far too long.

"Sorry, Sir."

"Hudson. And no need to apologize. I had the same expression when I saw it for the first time, and I've to say that it still happens to me." Hudson said as he walked towards the couch. Karen followed.

"So, tell me, Karen... I hope I can call you Karen?" Hudson was too polite for his stature.

"Sure," Karen said as she sat at the other end of the couch.

"So, Karen, tell me about this case of yours. This Sanchez person."

He had given her the space to speak, but she didn't know what to say or if she wanted to say anything at all. She had been vilified brutally over the last few months since the shooting.

"Okay, let me ask you a few basic questions to start with. Why didn't you accept the offer to settle this, out of the courthouse?"

"That will mean that I'm accepting that it was intentional. I'll be stained for life."

"Karen, I know people try to judge your actions on a decision that you made in 3 seconds. They think they can pour over what we have to do in lengthy court hearings and then arrive at options that they think we should have chosen. But if you put them in the same circumstances, 99 out of 100 times, they would do the same or even worse."

.   .   .

Karen said nothing, but she felt relieved that Hudson understood her predicament. Hudson waited for her to respond, but she said nothing. Just kept staring at her coffee mug.

"You know Karen, I grew up in the Englewood neighborhood of Chicago. The time was the early 1950s and the area, at that time, was a diverse and densely populated one that was just beginning to attract African American residents. As white families moved out, the percentage of African Americans soared through the 1950s to 1960s, from 11 percent in 1950 to 68 percent in 1960. At that time, I didn't know about these numbers. All I knew was that most of my friends were slowly moving out of the neighborhood. Mine was one of the white families that chose not to move. That was also the time when the construction on the Dan Ryan Expressway had cut a swath of destruction through the neighborhood. But, to me, Englewood was just a normal neighborhood. People tried to take care of their property. The kids I played with weren't in gangs, or anything like that," Hudson recalled.

"Everything was good until it wasn't. One evening, Tony, one of my friends, was stopped on his way home by a group of kids. He knew that they were gang members, he tried to run, but they grabbed him. He was stabbed 36 times.

*36 times.*

"I was nearby, and when I heard his cries, I ran to save him, but it was too late. I stayed with him until the first responder arrived. I saw them putting him on a stretcher. He took that last gasp. I was fifteen then. I remember because now I know what it means. That day I decided to be someone who could do something about such things. But I had no money; no one in my family had any money. To become anything, I had to save up the tuition, so I took a job bagging grocery. One of the cashiers had a brother who was a cop. The cop got to know me and one of the grocery clerks. One day, the officer suggested that we should sign up for the city's police cadet program. We would get training, tuition for college, and a paycheck—all in exchange for agreeing to work flexible hours with the police.

"The other guy signed up, but I was unsure. That was 1968. That summer, police officers had clashed with protesters at the Democratic National Convention in what some called 'a police riot.' Reverend Jesse Jackson had described Chicago Mayor Richard J. Daley as a fascist; groups such as the Chicago-based Nation of Islam were ridiculing the early civil rights movement's emphasis on nonviolence. I remember asking my friend why he wanted to be a policeman. He looked at me and said, 'What do you have against the police?'

"I thought about it. I liked the police officer I'd gotten to know bagging groceries. So, I made up my mind and signed up for the gig. Three years later, I exited the cadet program with a college degree and an assignment as an officer with the Chicago Police Department." Hudson looked at Karen, who was listening to him with rapt attention. "You must be thinking, why I'm telling you all this?" Hudson said while getting up leaving his cup.

· · ·

Karen didn't know how to respond to this but, partly, she wondered what this had to do with her situation. She followed his lead in getting up. The coffee was finished.

"You and I share many more things than you could ever imagine. I lost my mother at a very young age just like you did. Both of us come from a small town with dreams of making it big in this country. I've had my share of disappointments in my career, like the one you are facing now. It was never a rosy ride for me." Hudson moved towards his work-table and leaned against its edge. Karen stopped at a comfortable distance.

"Despite all the stumbling blocks, I have always loved this job. And the thing I loved the most is the action—the adrenaline that came from making a good 'pinch'. But it was one incident in particular that pushed me to think seriously about my future as a beat cop. One night, my partner and I had been called to the scene of a homicide involving a local drug dealer. The dealer was long dead. Two "wagon men"—older officers, both big guys, smoking cigars—arrived and went upstairs to the top floor of the flat to retrieve the body. When they came back, there was this boy with them, who might have been a protégé of the dead man, or maybe someone connected with the drug trade. I watched them struggle down the stairs, panting heavily, lit cigars pointing straight up to the night sky. The boy knew that those two could never catch him if he somehow succeeded in getting away from their grip. And he did get away, almost. The officers were unprepared, and the boy was free in an instant. One of the two older officers didn't know how to react to this sudden situation and, without thinking much, trained his gun to the boy's back and shot twice. I think it was the second bullet that hit the boy and, before anyone could do anything, he was dead. The officer was eventually tried in a court of law but, watching those two cops, I knew that's not who I wanted to become. So, I signed up to take the sergeant's exam the next day. Luckily, my timing was good. After decades of being segregated, the CPD was moving ahead in the direction of true integration. During the 1970s, the department embraced putting black and white officers in the same cars. 'Salt and peppers,' as they called them at that time. I made sergeant in 1977, lieutenant in 1984, before becoming commander of a district and then of the narcotics division. When Superintendent Roy Smith announced he was stepping down, I applied for the top job. But you know what, I didn't get the job. One of my colleagues did.

"But that was not the end of the road for me. The next month, I got a call from a headhunter asking if I'd be interested in applying for the position as a superintendent. He was looking for someone to turn around the troubled police department. Two board members flew to Chicago to talk with me. That spring, I took the job and moved to here. My family stayed in Chicago." While talking, Hudson had leisurely straightened himself and, suddenly, Karen found him standing too close. She had not moved, but Hudson had, and now was looking straight in her eyes while Karen had to raise her head to look back. She didn't know if she should take a step back or stay in the same position. She could smell Hudson—a mix of coffee, cigarette, and cologne. But even as her mind whirled, Hudson continued without apprehension. "When I came here, I found the police department to be a complete mess. It was a very dysfunctional, under-resourced and demoralized department. I've never worked in a third world country, but it had to be something like that. I had no clue if I'd succeed in turning it around. Just like you are thinking right now about whether or not you will get out of this mess."

．　．　．

Karen hadn't noticed it soon enough, but when she did, Hudson's right hand was already on her waist, moving down. She was dumbfounded by the turn of events, unsure of how to react.

Hudson saw Karen's expression changing yet continued as if nothing had happened. "The need of the hour is to create part-nerships among police officers to identify issues that contribute to crime and solve them. Karen, you must maintain close contacts with certain people and understand how fragile these relationships really can be. One wrong decision can jeopardize your entire worldview." Hudson stopped speaking, but his eyes never left Karen's. His lips curled into a microscopic smile as he loosened his grip, letting Karen go free. She quickly got away from Hudson.

"Karen, you are beautiful. There are few like you in the force. I'm sure you must be proud of that."

Karen didn't respond. Her face was red with anger. She turned quickly to get out of the room.

"I spoke to Judge Anderson."

Karen stopped at the door, her hand on the doorknob.

．　．　．

"He doesn't like you. The jury doesn't trust you. It looks like your father will be hugely disappointed soon. Watching his pride shatter will be painful, won't it? I'd be disappointed, too. Nobody, especially me, wants to lose an asset like you for killing a Mexican. It would be a shame."

Karen turned around.

"You know, I can get you out of this mess," Hudson breathed without hurrying. His voice was calm and in control. It was either his confidence as the top cop of the state or as someone who had done this time and again with others. Karen knew what was coming next, yet she remained standing there. A lot of things on her mind stopped her from dashing out of the place.

"On the eve of Christmas, there is a huge party planned for the whole department at Cilly's. You will get an invitation to attend that party and you will go there. But you won't stay long. You will make an excuse and meet me at your precinct. If you come, I'll take care of you. If you don't, then..." He smiled, leaving his words hanging in the air. "You can go now. I've work to do." Hudson concluded as if cutting a cord with a snap.

Karen remained standing, staring at the door. She could hear Hudson slowly walking to his chair. She heard him getting back to the file he was reading earlier. She stayed there for a second longer and then with a beaten look, turned the doorknob.

"Wear something nice," Hudson spoke from behind. Karen knew

that he was now checking out her rear. "Close the door softly."
He said. She could imagine him smiling again. The smile of a
victor.

Karen wanted to slam the door, yet she couldn't. She didn't
know what stopped her from doing it.

# CHAPTER 7

Karen didn't take the elevator down. She walked down the stairs. Her mind was blank, trying to process what had just happened. Was it her mistake? Did she give some kind of indication to Hudson to make a move on her? Why had her body stopped reacting when it was happening? She could still feel Hudson's hand moving on her body like a snake. She wanted to walk, move, digest, ingest, cry.

She kept walking.

There are moments in life when you know you've crossed a bridge and your old life is over. This meeting was her bridge.

She stepped off the curb. Her tears blinded her, but she kept walking. She was stepping off another curb, God knows where.

.   .   .

An hour later, she found herself on some deserted road. She finally stopped, shivering. She didn't know where she was or how far she had walked, but she didn't want to stop. Her legs hurt like hell, but her mind was screaming at her to keep walking. She didn't know what time it was, but it was dark. Real dark. She checked her cell phone. The blue light shone like a star in the deserted street. It was half-past one in the night.

She had been walking for the last four hours.

# CHAPTER 8

## Earlier that Day

Karen looked at her image in the mirror. The girl staring back at her looked unreal. Karen had always been a looker, but her job and her aversion to standing out based on her features made her dress in the simplest of clothes and use minimal or no makeup. This, despite her being an expert in applying makeup during her teen years. But tonight, she wanted to look gorgeous. Not for anyone else, but for herself. Tonight would also be the night when her problems would either go away or amplify with renewed ferocity. Either way, she would take them head-on while looking stunning. Wearing a short red dress and high heels, she gave herself a sublime touch with deft, if slightly rusty, hands. The backless dress amply showed her assets. She had made sure that anyone would fall for her tonight.

She checked her cell and found that the cab was still five minutes away. She opened her purse and checked it one last time. Everything she needed was in it. She had meticulously prepared for the night and was satisfied with the result. Her destination was Gilly's Grill and Bar, where the annual party was happening. The whole New Jersey Police department was expected to be there, without their families—a testosterone-filled gathering of law enforcement personnel who would be on their best worst behavior, all night long. Though she didn't have to bear with it long; Hudson had asked her to leave the party in an hour or so and meet him at the precinct which would probably be deserted. She didn't know why he chose her station, but she didn't ask. She had decided what she had to do and why she had to do it. There was no turning back now. Her phone rang. It was the cab driver.

Putting on her velvet overcoat, she checked the living room one last time and locked the door behind her. Hiding the key beneath the third flowerpot from the door for her roommate, who had gone out for a dinner date with one of her co-workers and forgotten to take her own key, she walked towards the elevator.

Stepping out onto the pavement, she instantly felt the biting cold on her face. Instinctively, she tightened her posture and looked at the only car near the building, meant for her. The driver was waiting for her. She walked towards it and opened the door. Before sliding in, she observed the black sky. It would probably snow tonight, she thought and boarded the cab.

The ride was going to take forty-five minutes. The good thing was that Karen wasn't in any hurry. Since she met Hudson six days ago, she had spent a lot of time thinking about her options. Off work, confined to her cramped apartment, eating and sleeping and watching the world in motion from her window while she sat still, she had a lot of time to think about and consider everything. In the cab, she was so engrossed in her thoughts she didn't keep track of time. The ringing of the phone interrupted her train of thought. She checked it and found that it was an unknown number. She still picked up.

"On your way to the party?" the voice asked.

"Yes." She knew who was on the other side. The voice was unmistakably his.

"You know the bakery, My Daughter's Cakes?"

"Yes."

"Get down there. A BMW will wait for you."

"But Sir." Karen was surprised at the sudden change of plan.

"Karen, I told you to call me Hudson. Meet me there." Hudson sniggered and disconnected the call.

"Drop me at the 'My Daughter's Cakes' bakery." Karen told the driver.

.  .  .

Karen waited for the cab to leave before walking towards the only vehicle parked near the bakery. She knocked on the driver's side window and found a familiar set of eyes looking back at her. Without saying anything, Samara unlocked the back door and signaled Karen to get inside. Karen asked nothing, even though she wanted to. Hudson was using Samara, his personal assistant, to get to the girls but, more importantly, what made Samara agree to this? Why was she doing it? Samara pressed the accelerator, and the BMW lurched forward.

Except for the first hiccup, Samara proved to be a deft driver. The BMW sped along the empty streets effortlessly. Neither of them felt the need to speak to each other. They were both doing things they shouldn't be, and yet here they were. Only they and their God knew what made them agree to be a part of it.

Karen checked her cell. It was 10:25 p.m. She had been traveling for almost an hour and didn't even know where she was going. The last-minute change was worrying, but then again, what could be worse than her current situation? She looked out of the window and found the surroundings familiar. She was on the same street where her station was—their earlier meeting place for tonight, but not anymore. She observed the station building fading away, but Samara didn't make any effort to slow down. The journey ended soon afterward, though. The BMW sped a couple of blocks further down and then turned into an alley.

*Pelican Motel.*

.   .   .

Samara slowly brought the BMW to a halt and unlocked Karen's side of the door. Karen knew what Samara wanted and got out of the car. Without looking at her, Samara geared the BMW in the reverse to get out of the alley. The place was the backside of the Pelican motel. It was one of those places where Karen expected the next crime to occur. Despite being close to the station, she had not been here ever before.

Standing in that dark alley alone, in a tiny red dress, hundreds of uneasy feelings crossed her mind. What if someone attacked her? She didn't have her gun. Standing there, she was thinking hard about what she should do next when her phone rang.

"Get in. Use the back door." It was from Hudson. Samara must have informed him.

Using her cellphone's weak flashlight, she looked around for the door. And then she saw it. She grabbed the door's handle and pulled. As the door opened, the light from inside spilled out into the alley. Without pausing for thought, she got in. Whatever she would have to face on the other side would be better than where she was right now. She closed the door behind her and settled her nerves. She had not noticed it earlier, but her breathing had accelerated in the darkness of the back alley. Once calm, she looked around. She was standing in a poorly lit long corridor.

"Walk." Hudson was still on the phone. Hearing his voice brought Karen back to her reality. The thought of why she was here started to haunt her again.

. . .

Yet she walked.

At the end of the corridor, she could see a door. She opened it and found herself in the reception area of the motel. There was a reception counter standing next to the door from which she had just exited. The man behind the counter looked at her with indifference and slid a key towards her.

*Room 215.*

She looked back at him and found him gesturing towards the elevators near the stairs. It was very well orchestrated, as if she was in a live-footage kind of movie, with cameras hidden, tracking her every step. She didn't know how her face would have looked just then, but the prominent expression would likely be one of shock.

She didn't know if asking this man questions would amount to anything, so she moved towards the elevators. The elevator car was already on the first floor, ready for her, but she had to pause. She didn't know which floor she had to go. As soon as this crossed her mind, she looked back at the man and found him still watching her.

"Third floor. Take left. Last room."

Mechanically she walked inside the elevator car and pressed three. The doors closed at their own pace while she stood silently. On the third floor, she turned left as told and walked towards the end of the hallway. On her right was room 215. She knocked.

"Come in." She heard Hudson's voice from inside the room and twisted the doorknob. Inside, a foyer led to a large room. She walked inside and closed the door unhurriedly. The room smelled aromatic. The lighting was dim. As she appeared in the large space beyond the foyer, her eyes found Hudson, sitting in his bathrobe on a large chair kept at the end of the double bed, watching her keenly. A bottle of sparkling wine shone on a sturdy wooden table beside his chair. She couldn't read the name on the bottle but, by the shape of it, the wine looked expensive.

"Keep your bag there." Hudson instructed.

Karen looked at the wall-mounted shelf and put her purse on it.

"Come here."

She obeyed.

"Drop your dress." Hudson was in complete control and this was how he wanted it to be. Karen flinched at the command. Hudson waited for her to obey while staring directly into her kohl-lined eyes. The humiliation was getting worse, but Karen had thought through everything a million times before coming here. She was ready for anything. After a few extra seconds, Karen started to loosen her dress. Watching her do that, Hudson got up from his place and, with his right hand, undid his bathrobe.

"Those as well." He said, looking at Karen's innerwear. Karen slowly got rid of them, too.

Hudson inched forward and stopped at the edge of the bed. "Come here." Karen covered the rest of the distance.

"Wine?" he asked, as she paused at a comfortable distance.

Karen nodded and Hudson poured two glasses.

"More." Karen spoke for the first time.

Hudson looked at her and then filled the glass meant for her.

"Do you have ice?" She asked.

"With wine?" Hudson sounded surprised.

"Yes." she replied flatly.

Hudson wasn't prepared for this, but he hoped that the hotel refrigerator would have some. Instead of instructing Karen to get it, he oddly decided to do it himself. He walked towards the refrigerator and opened it. It had ice cubes. For how long they had been there he didn't know and certainly didn't care.

Karen watched Hudson lumbering to the mini-refrigerator. As the light fell properly on the 63-year-old, she saw a body that was frail and failing. Hudson didn't know he was being watched. Karen examined his back while he checked the refrigerator for ice and felt a strange aversion. Hudson turned around and walked back towards the table. She turned her head to the other side. It was hard to watch him without feeling nauseated.

Hudson put the ice down on the table and turned to face Karen, but he knew something had changed. He could see it in her eyes.

"How many?" he asked her about the cubes.

"Couple of." She responded, trying hard to hide her hate for him.

He dropped two and offered her the glass. She took it. Hudson turned to take his glass when Karen jerked her hand. The ice cubes hit Hudson's face first and then the wine. He recoiled, his hands coming up to cover his face. Karen threw her glass on the carpeted floor and grabbed Hudson's neck from behind, bringing it down fiercely. Blinded and shocked, Hudson couldn't offer any resistance and his skull hit the corner of the wooden table with extreme force. His entire world appeared to collapse, and he fell on his knees.

Next, Karen grabbed the wine bottle and smashed it on the table, breaking it from the middle. She then swung her hand, and the broken bottle pierced Hudson's right arm. He screamed with all his might.

"What the fuck!" he yelled. "Help me." He was crying.

She then pulled the bottle out and stepped back. Hudson yelled louder. She didn't care what the old man was spitting at her. Her mind was occupied. She quickly grabbed her purse and took out a large poly bag, throwing the bloodied bottle into it. She then came back and grabbed her wineglass, and put it in the bag, too. She then went into the restroom and washed the blood off her hands. Quickly putting on her dress, she took out a cotton cloth and wrapped it around her right hand. She had to remove her fingerprints from everything she had touched in the room. Hudson was still on the floor, flopping in a pool of his own blood, yelling for help. She looked at him with abhorrence before closing the door behind her.

She wanted to hurt him, but not kill him.

Hudson couldn't admit to meeting Karen here and he would always be afraid that she wouldn't hesitate to tell all if there was ever an inquiry. In all senses, that would be the end of Hudson's legacy. She knew, however, that Hudson would not leave her alone. She was still on the losing side of the case and this would just escalate her downfall in the department. He would use all the leverage he had to make sure she would be gone forever. She could blackmail him, but she didn't know to what extent and for how long. It was her only option, though she was reluctant to use it. She would have to think about it soon but, right now, she had to get out of there.

The third-floor corridor was still deserted. The rooms seemed to be unoccupied, at least on this floor. Hudson had chosen the room smartly. No other guests meant there would be no witnesses. Karen didn't wait for the elevator but took the stairs. On her way up, she had seen the main entry door that opened onto the main street. That was the best way out. The only problem might be the man at the reception, but she didn't care.

As she descended the stairs, she normalized her walk. No bloodstains on her, she had made sure of that. She was coming off unharmed and untouched. What she felt inside, however, was a different matter. No one could tell that that she was shaken and fidgety inside for sure until she gave them a chance.

The reception was deserted. The man had gone, possibly for a smoke or to sleep. She didn't care. The wall clock behind the reception table told her that the night was approaching twelve. She got out of the building and stepped into the deserted main street. It was badly lit, but still better than the dark back alley.

# CHAPTER 9

She checked her cell. No cabs. She had to walk, there was no other option.

But she had to run. Someone from the motel might come looking for her soon.

Her high heels didn't do her any good. She again checked the cab-hailing app on her cell. No cabs near her. She kept inching away from the building. Every step in those heels was a struggle. Half an hour later, she still wasn't very far from the precinct. The fear of getting ambushed from behind was clouding her judgment with each step. What if Hudson's men or Samara grabbed her from behind? What would she do then? She didn't have her gun with her. It had been seized by the department because of the court case. She thought of taking her heels off but being barefoot on the concrete road would only slow her down further. She was still deciding when she heard them.

. . .

Faint footsteps. She hesitated and looked back. The footsteps stopped. Quick as a thought, she turned around. No one. She wasn't imagining things. Someone was there. She was sure of that. She increased her speed. The footsteps resurfaced. Hastened. She stopped and swiftly looked back. Still no one. She turned and started to sprint, barefoot. The concrete road made her wince with each step. The footsteps sped up. She didn't look back this time.

Not far from her, a streetlamp was flickering. Underneath it, a Toyota was parked. Maybe she could get some help. But she still had to cross a dark alley to reach there.

She could scream. She could scream for help. Her mouth opened. Her right hand rose involuntarily.

But before she could say a word, an arm grabbed her from behind, seizing her throat and nipping her cry in the bud. Something sharp pierced the back of her neck. And before she could try to free herself, she crumpled face down on the ground like a tossed-out paper in the bin. Lying on the ground, as her eyes drooped shut, she saw a shadow standing next to her.

# CHAPTER 10

Loud ringing. Somebody's phone was ringing.

The back of her closed eyes was bright. Loud ringing again. The smell was gone. She opened her eyes. The burlap had been removed.

She was in a room. It was a large hall with a very high roof, much like in a warehouse, with a lot of steel shelves. She felt her hands —they were free. She was still sitting on the chair but not bound by any ropes. Her head ached, but at least she was free. She was still in the same red dress and high heels.

To her left was a door. Open. She got up and immediately stumbled. Her legs were still recovering from the tight leash. Why was she free? Who abducted her? All those questions were still in the air but she had to get out of here first. Whoever abducted her would come back soon, and she had to get out before. She gathered every inch of her strength and made her way to the door.

Adrenaline rushed back through her veins as she started to move. Slowly, she was gaining back her stride. She moved cautiously, without making a sound; ready for anything. As soon as she walked out the door, she found herself in an aisle with racks of clothes lined across the walls. She turned to her right first to check the hallway. But when an unknown hand grabbed her left shoulder, she reacted instinctively. Without looking in that direction; she raised her left arm, freeing her shoulder from the grip. Her right fist followed closely, landing forcefully on the lower part of the man's breastbone. The man wasn't ready for the assault and couldn't absorb the hard blow. Karen's right arm recoiled, and then her fist swung back with the same force, hitting his breastbone at the center this time, breaking a few of his ribs. The man this time stumbled backwards, unable to regain his balance. Karen looked around and found a movable aluminum ladder. She grabbed it with both hands and slammed its far end into the man's skull. There was a cracking sound. She crouched and hit the ladder's end on his knees. The man was now flat on the floor. She threw down the ladder and grabbed the closest rack and pulled it forward to fall on to the man, giving him no chance to come back with an answer.

She paused to check the corridor. The walls were lined with ceiling-height racks, with overcoats and clothes on them. A few of the overcoats were also hanging in the court racks. She checked the closest one to her and luckily found a bunch of keys. She hastened down the same hallway from which the man had appeared. The corridor was dimly lit, with a light bulb hanging in the middle and fighting the darkness. Keys in her right fist, she ran towards the other end. There had to be a door somewhere in there. She was near the light bulb when a man stepped into the hallway, some thirty yards away from her, making her stop in her tracks.

Her grip tightened around the keys. The pointed blade of the key was pointing out between her fingers.

"Where are you going?" The man asked calmly.

"Who are you?"

"None of your business." He moved cautiously towards her.

"Did Hudson send you?"

"You'll know soon." He was now dangerously close, so she threw the first punch, aiming the blade of the key towards his left eye. The man was ready. He grabbed Karen's shooting arm with both hands and moved his body away from the line of attack. His left hand grabbed her wrist and his right hand was on her arm. He jerked her unstable body and pushed her forward. Freeing his right arm, he grabbed the back of her neck, making her wince with pain. In three moves, he was on top, and that was his first mistake. Karen used her opponent's momentum as he attacked and kept on with the rotation, crouching during the middle of the turn. The man wasn't ready for this and his grip on Karen's neck loosened. She pulled herself away from the attacker and freed herself from his grip.

In the next second, her left fist landed squarely on the left side of his rib cage. He was taken aback by the agility of his opponent. Karen followed her first successful punch with another left punch to his face, but the man blocked it with his right hand and grabbed her arm again. With his left hand, he grabbed her neck and pulled her closer.

She grunted.

He smiled.

Their bodies swayed in tandem, moving clockwise. The man led. Karen had to follow. Karen jerked her hands away from the attacker, again freeing herself from his grip. The man stumbled. The girl was faster than he had expected.

But he could praise her later because Karen had already thrown a right punch and the key's blade swung at the man's face. He jerked away and Karen missed. She threw a left punch at his face and he jerked away. Missed again. She changed tactics, and this time aimed for his stomach, connecting this time. The key's blade could have punctured his stomach, but his jacket saved him. Karen came back quickly with a follow-up punch to the man's face, but he used his left hand to block it. Another right punch, but the man ducked this time. Karen was out of breath. The man had been waiting for this. Her next punch was weak, and he again grabbed her arm and neck, pulling her closer. His hand knocked into her head. His hands tightened on her neck but he missed the punch coming from beneath, making it through the space between his arms. The fist connected with the lower part of his jaw and his head jerked back. She took this opportunity to get out of his grip.

Once free, she clutched her hands together and, with a Hammer throw, smashed a massive punch into his face. The man stumbled back wildly. She quickly saw the opportunity and kicked his left knee, only to be immediately surprised. The man had not only handled the blow successfully but had gotten back to his feet in no time. But it would still not be enough because Karen had positioned the key's blade in her right hand again and swung it towards his left cheek. The key pierced the man's soft skin and got stuck. The man's smile was gone. The bunch clanked as he got back to his feet. He pulled it out without hesitation. Karen was out of breath and couldn't escape when the man stormed at her like a raging bull, blood dripping from his cheek.

He grabbed Karen's neck and slammed her body into the wall behind her, forcing the air out of her lungs. She gagged, but the man's grip only tightened. Her legs, hanging in the air, tried to hit something but failed. In the light of the only bulb, her eyes rested on the man's glowing face. She had seen him before, but where?

# CHAPTER 11

"That's enough." A voice reverberated in the hallway. The man's grip loosened and then, as if she was a doll, he brought Karen back to the ground. As soon as her feet touched the floor, he backed away from her. He was still attentive but not hostile, as if someone had flicked a switch in him. Karen didn't understand any of this, but she was still wary of the man who, a second ago, had almost killed her.

"Karen, we would like to talk to you. Mark, please escort Ms. Karen to the briefing room."

Karen looked at the man who was just trying to kill her. He nodded his head and moved towards the door from which he had appeared.

"Who are you?" Karen remained where she was. She would not follow orders from a disembodied voice. There wasn't any response. The man waited for Karen to join him at the door. He was observing her as if this was the most reasonable thing to do in that place and he had seen enough people in the same situation, weighing their options.

"You coming?" He asked.

Karen remained in place, thinking hard. The man waited for a couple of seconds before disappearing into the darkness beyond the door.

"Shit," Karen muttered under her breath and followed him. Her curiosity had finally gotten the best of her. The door led her to a room. The man wasn't there, but the room was brighter than the corridor outside because of a light spilling into the room from a second door to her left. Karen followed the light and found that the door led to a long narrow corridor with multiple doors on both sides. Unlike the one she was coming from, this hallway was well lit, though the peeling paint still made sure it had something in common with the rest of the building.

She stepped into the hallway and immediately felt as though the air had become lighter and fresher. There was no foul smell either. In fact, there was no smell at all. Her eyes scanned the confined space as she slowly walked down the hallway. What she didn't notice was that the door behind her had been noiselessly shut and, as soon as it was closed, another door in the hallway opened. The man whom she followed reappeared at that door. He looked at her. Her apprehensive posture was telling of her mental state. He waited for her without saying a word. She paused for a moment and then looked back. The door from where she came from was shut. She didn't know when, but going back and checking it if it would open would have been foolish. She had taken a leap of faith and her gut was telling her to move forward. She was still not ready to see what lay ahead, but it was her gut feeling that made her move along.

Considering every option available to her, which, in reality, were not many, she turned back to face the man and walked to the open door. Once closer, the man motioned her to go inside. It was another room with a chair and a wooden table at its center.

"Karen, please take a seat." The same modulated voice sounded through the room through two tiny but powerful speakers.

Karen looked back at the man who stared back at her indifferently. She then looked back at the setting in front of her. The room was an interrogation room and this time; she was on the wrong side of it.

"I'm good." She spoke to the voice, not knowing how it would be construed. She was in unfamiliar territory with no knowledge of the ground rules. But this was also a way to test the waters on how much latitude she could negotiate from the voice.

"As you please." The voice didn't take offense. "Mark, please close the door."

. . .

The man closed the door and walked across the room to stand at the opposite corner. His hands were folded, and his gaze was fixed on Karen. Karen walked across the room and positioned herself at a comfortable distance from Mark. Two close circuit television cameras mounted at two corners of the concrete roof rotated and then, after a slight adjustment, glared at Karen. Their whirring sounds seemed weird in the silent room. Karen saw them coming to a standstill.

"Where am I?" Karen fired the first shot, looking at Mark. She had already had enough of this veiled secrecy and abduction.

"You are in a secure facility in New Jersey." The response came from the voice.

"Why am I here?"

"My team thinks you're a good prospect for the work we do."

"What kind of work?" Karen was getting bolder, but the voice didn't oblige her with a response.

"What team is this?" Unperturbed by the silence, Karen fired another question, which again met with no response.

"Who are you?" She asked next.

.  .  .

"You don't need to know that." The voice responded this time.

"Then I'd prefer to get out of here."

"I wouldn't do that if I were you." The voice said.

"Who will stop me?" Karen blurted out, venting all her bottled-up anger.

"No one. If you want to go, then trust me, I'll be glad. Despite my team's recommendation of you, in my opinion, you are still very much a work in progress, which may or may not reach its zenith. It'd be a headache to train a resource who might never be used in the field." The voice was calm.

Karen said nothing. The option of leaving anytime she wanted was unexpected and had caught her off guard. But it also hurt her ego.

"You are fighting a lost case and, considering what you have done to Hudson, your career in the New Jersey Police department is almost over. You might have been one of the top rankers in the academy or a hero at your old job, but in your current job, you have done nothing, accomplished nothing. To make sure that this will remain the story of your life, Hudson will make sure that you will be dragged into long court cases about attacking a superintendent and breaking the police code of conduct. And when all this will be over, whatever you've earned in your insignificant career will be tarnished beyond recognition. Your father, who is proud of you, might still love you, but I don't think he will be able to withstand the pressure Hudson and America's judicial system will put on him and his daughter. So, you can leave anytime, but the question is where will you go?" There was no mockery, just a simple statement of facts. Everything going on in Karen's mind was laid bare by the person behind the voice. And she still did not understand about whom or what she was dealing with. She was at an enormous disadvantage with almost no negotiating power in this conversation.

"Karen, I know what you are thinking." The voice said.

*Do you?* Karen thought, but said nothing.

"This world is a terrible place and we all have problems that seem insurmountable to us. But there are bigger predicaments. Problems which, if not solved ahead of time, will lead to mass destruction, murders, and faltering economies. There are no random acts in this chaotic world, except for us forgetting our car keys. There are organizations and agencies working overtime to topple America and its allies. And despite the alphabet soup of agencies we have, we are still always two steps behind the schemers and perpetrators of these acts. That's because to stop them, we need to be like them, think like them, and act like them. No government will ever authorize any of its agencies to function like this in an ideal world. Unfortunately, we don't live in an ideal world. This world is fucked beyond recognition and we are just about surviving it. It's mine and my team's job to rein in this chaos and take care of American interests and Americans while working in the shadows."

. . .

"What do you call this team?"

"Task Force-77. You will not find us anywhere. Like I said, in an ideal world, we don't exist."

"What do you want from me?"

"As I mentioned, my team saw some potential in you. Your abduction was a test to make sure everyone knows what you can do and where you need training. My team will make sure that we harness your skills to keep this country safe. The best people in this country will train you but, if you fail, you will go back to your old life, or maybe a completely new life. If you pass, then you will get a new life and your father will be taken care of for the rest of his life by the U.S. government. Now, the question is what you want, and you have to choose now."

"What if I say yes? What happens then?"

"Mark will escort you to a secure training facility after you sign a few papers."

"What about the people in the department, my father, my belongings?"

. . .

"To them, you will be dead. My team will find a reason and a way to do it. You will get a new identity."

"So, I cannot meet my father ever."

"Accepting this job means that you will have to leave people behind. Even if you fail the training, you cannot meet or see him. This is a one-way street, from here."

"What about Hudson?"

"What about him?"

"The way he did what he did, I'm sure I'm not the first one whom he did this to. Someone has to make sure that he can't get away from his deeds."

"What do you have in mind?"

"I don't know, but I want him removed from society."

"We don't kill people for revenge, and neither can you, even if you don't join us. I'll make sure of that. The law of the land has to be upheld."

.   .   .

"If I have to leave my family and my friends for a life where everything is uncertain, then this is my one condition." Karen was taking a huge gamble with the meager options that she had. But whoever these people were, they had gone to great lengths to convince her to stay and join them. She looked at Mark, whose blank gaze gave her no sign if what she had asked was even worth considering.

The silence that ensued was far longer than she had expected. Her thoughts were running in multiple directions, from imagining that her file was being re-analyzed to her usefulness being a topic back on the discussion table. This also gave her some time to weigh her options. Not being able to see her father was one thing but being dead to him was a different thing altogether. He only had her. Her mother had left them when she was eight and, since then, she was his everything.

But a dead daughter was still significantly better than seeing her getting humiliated in the public courts. They didn't have the means to take on people like Hudson head-on. She knew that if it came to that, her chances of winning would be extremely low. Her faith in the American justice system was bleak, despite being a law enforcement personnel. But the things she would lose were huge—her father's happiness, her own reputation, her savings, her benefits, her 401K, and so much more. By choosing this, though she would at least be able to serve her country, and they would take care of her father, even if she wasn't there.

She felt like crying, but couldn't here. Her efforts still failed, and her eyes became moist. She lowered her head as if she was thinking of something deeply and then casually raised her hands, rubbing her face, eyes, and forehead as if she was trying to keep herself alert. Once sure that her tears were wiped away, she raised her head and, from the corner of her eye, checked on Mark. He was still in the same place, alert and expressionless.

After a silence of over fifteen minutes, the voice reverberated in the room again. "If we agree to your condition, then you have to sign a special contract with us."

"What special contract?"

"Legal will share the details with you once you let us know your decision. Now is the time for it, so what is it?"

Karen was in a fix. She had already taken the leap of faith once she put forth her conditions, but these last few steps of the journey still made her pause.

"The offer won't last forever." The voice pushed her.

"I agree." Karen blurted out.

"Mark, please take Karen to her house for now. She will be moved to the facility on Wednesday night. Explain the protocol that she has to follow until her transfer." The voice ordered Mark, who just nodded his head.

·   ·   ·

"Karen, we don't accept any deviation from the protocols so closely listen to Mark and follow his every word. Any deviation will jeopardize your successful relocation and this arrangement. My team doesn't leave any loose ends so if you deviate from the plan, then we will have no other option but to eliminate you. Do not contact anyone until further notice, not even your father. Mark will tell you what you need to do next." This time, the instructions were for her.

Karen nodded. Wednesday was three days away.

# CHAPTER 12

As soon as the voice stopped, Mark took out his cell phone. He pressed some keys and the wall opposite to the door made a noise. Then, as if a lever had turned inside the wall, a small square-shaped box moved back and slid left. Mark looked at Karen and found her looking surprised. Without saying anything, he walked towards the new exit and ducked to get through it. Karen looked around. There was no one in the room but the cameras were still pointed at her. She was still being watched. Without thinking too much about it, she followed Mark. Once she got to the other side, the box slid back to its original position. If no one looked closely enough, it was just a wall.

She looked around. This was a bigger room, with better lighting. The walls were white, making it look like a hospital, but she knew better.

"This way." Mark signaled to his right. This time, it was her turn to lead. She was still wary of him, but the way he looked at her left her with no choice. Mark was walking a step behind her.

"You fight well." He suddenly spoke, making Karen miss a step. A stumbling thank you escaped her lips.

"They'll make you better."

"Who?" she asked this time; she was interested. Maybe this Mark wasn't so smug and closed as he seemed to her.

"The instructors." He said nothing further. Karen waited, then changed the topic.

"What is this Task Force-77?"

"A Black ops team." He gave an answer that Karen already knew. She wanted more.

"Who runs it?"

"I don't know. All I know is that not even the U.S. President can tell them how to execute their missions."

"What about you?"

.  .  .

"I'm in the recruitment team."

"So, you chose me."

"That is the job of another team. They brought you here to test your skills."

"So, there are more like you in this team."

"Like me? No, Better."

"Better than you?" Karen was surprised. Mark was a good fighter and could easily hold his own against a competent fighter.

"Yes. I couldn't get through the last leg of the training, so I had limited options to choose from."

"What happens if you fail the first leg?"

"No idea. Trainee reports are confidential, so no one knows the final recommendation, but they tell you your options at the end of the training. And who could be a better judge of your own performance than you?"

. . .

They walked for twenty minutes through various corridors and then stepped in front of a large door. Mark took out an oversized sack mask from his back pocket and handed it to Karen. He said nothing, but it was clear what he wanted Karen to do. She took it without question and wore it, covering her face. He tightened the surrounding strap, though making sure she didn't suffocate. It was still better than the mask they forced on her earlier. She then stood still while Mark used a combination of a retina scan and a code to open the gate. A gyrating sound meant that the door had accepted the code.

"I have to hold your hand to take you to the car." Mark said politely. Karen extended her left hand and felt Mark's rough palm gripping it softly.

After walking for ten minutes, they stopped. Mark took out car keys and pushed a button on the key fob. The button sent a 40-bit code along with a function code, telling the car what it should do. Opening the passenger side door of the front row, he helped Karen get in and strap on her seat belt. Then coming back to the driver's seat, he fastened his own seat belt and started the engine. The engine made a smooth sound, and Karen soon felt the car gaining acceleration. Sitting in the car, Karen tried to guess the distance from the facility to her house but then considered that Mark would probably take additional turns and unconventional routes to her house. It was common sense and she would have done the same. After approximately two hours of travel, the car stopped.

. . .

"You can take off your mask," Mark ordered. Karen complied. Coming from darkness to light, her eyes took some time to adjust. She checked the car. It was a BMW. She watched Mark, opening his side of the door.

She checked her purse and found her apartment keys. Standing outside the car, she looked at him.

"You're coming with me?"

"No, I'm good. Just remember no contact with anyone and don't go outside. Order any groceries you need online. I'll be in touch with you once your relocation plan is ready."

"What about Hudson?" Karen shot the parting question.

"One thing at a time, but a plan will already be in the works when we talk next, and we'll talk soon."

They shook hands and Mark got behind the steering wheel. Karen checked the car, but there was no license plate on the vehicle.

# CHAPTER 13

Two Days Later

The water lay still in the bathtub that was filled up to the brim with ice cubes. Bubbles were forming and bursting on the surface as if coming from an air vent hidden beneath the surface. Suddenly, the liquid moved and Karen appeared, breaking the stillness of the icy water.

Her strong athletic body was a patchwork of bruises and cuts from the fight a couple of days ago. The pain had subsidized, but she needed a quick fix to ease the rest of it fast. Stepping away from the cold water, she pulled a towel across her body and poured two fingers of vodka into a glass. She looked down at the label and then to the mirror. She opened the vanity drawer. Next to the cosmetics was a framed photo of her and her father in front of a blue country house. She stared down at the photo for a moment, held by memory, before reaching for a compact. Slowly, she started to cover her contusions with makeup and then dressed in a navy crepe wool skirt suit, with heels and sunglasses. Simple and sexy.

She pulled a cigarette from the pack, stepping out of the bathroom. She glanced at her empty bed and lit her cigarette. And then she walked out of her apartment door.

Outside, Mark was waiting for her in an SUV. A bag was waiting for her in the back seat. As she opened the bag, she saw a Glock at rest. She checked the weapon. It was loaded, and awaiting her command.

# CHAPTER 14

Mark was in the driver's seat and Karen was sitting behind him. Their eyes scanned the theater's gate. As per their information, Hudson should be out of the theater by this time. It was ten at night. Hudson had a flight in a couple of hours, so he needed to be at the airport by eleven. But they had no option other than to wait in silence. Both were alert and wanted this to end as soon as possible. They were here for Hudson—the superintendent of the New Jersey Police force—and that meant that, if anything went wrong, the fallouts would be unimaginable, especially for Karen. But despite Mark's reservations, she had decided to go ahead with the plan.

She was only worried about one thing: what if Mark flipped at the last moment? This was her second meeting with him, and she still knew almost nothing about the man. Suddenly, as if a train had reached its destination, the theatre doors opened and a flurry of people started to leave the theater building. Amidst all this, they had to find Hudson. Two pairs of eyes scanned the crowd like crazy. And then she saw him.

.  .  .

"There." She pointed. Mark saw him too—Hudson, walking away from them. He softly pressed the accelerator and SUV lurched ahead. He kept a 30-yard distance between the SUV and Hudson, who was on foot and now looking for a taxi. Once the crowd thinned, Hudson had still not been successful in getting a cab. Standing not far away from the theater, he checked his watch and then looked back at the street, searching for any cab. Nothing. He looked frustrated. He then took out his cell phone and called someone.

"We need to move, now!"

"How?"

"Offer him a lift," Karen said from behind.

"What?"

"That's the only way. He doesn't know you. Tell him you work for the department." She quickly gave him a primer on what he should say to gain Hudson's trust and get him in the vehicle voluntarily. Mark was wary of the plan, but maybe she was right. Whoever Hudson had called would arrive soon. He gradually increased the speed and then slowed the SUV as it neared Hudson. Karen slouched in the back seat.

.  .  .

"Chief." Mark opened his side of the window and spoke loudly to get Hudson's attention. He was still engrossed in his phone.

"Yes?"

"Sergeant Charles Mckenzie. We met at the ball, sir."

Hudson looked confused, but Mark's confidence made him believe his story.

"Are you waiting for someone?" Mark asked.

"I have to catch a flight and I've called someone to drop me at the airport."

"No issues, if you are in a hurry, I can drop you. My house is near the airport."

"No… no, Sergeant. I don't want to trouble you." Hudson now sounded calmer.

"No trouble, Chief. In fact, it would be an honor. Let me help you with your luggage?"

.   .   .

"Just this bag. I prefer traveling light." Hudson gestured to his leather attaché case.

"Great." Mark opened his side of the door and got out. He then scurried to the other side of the SUV and opened the front passenger door. Hudson, who liked the gesture, walked to him with a smile. Sitting in the dark, Karen stared at Hudson. Her body was tense, and she felt a surge of anger rush through her body.

Hudson slid inside the SUV and Mark slowly closed the door. He then ran back to the driver's side and took his position behind the wheel.

"You said something about someone coming to pick you up. Do you want us to wait for them?" Mark asked politely.

"No, no… we must rush, I will inform them." Hudson said, looking at his cell.

"Sure." Mark sped up amidst the thin traffic.

"Yes, I got a ride…. No need to come… I'll call you once I reach the airport… Thanks." Hudson spoke briefly on the phone.

Once they reached the main route, the traffic thinned further.

Mark drove in silence. Hudson was looking ahead when his cell chimed.

"It's a remarkable time to be in America." He said, reading a text.

"I agree."'

"The music, nightlife, and great restaurants. You've got any suggestions?"

"I'm a novice in these areas, Chief," Mark responded without looking at Hudson. "She might have some though."

"Who?" Hudson asked.

"Hello, Hudson," Karen spoke from behind him. Her Glock was pointed at his back. "I know a place you would be interested in."

Hudson saw Karen's face in the rear-view mirror and flinched, trying to turn back.

"Don't." She pressed the Glock's barrel against his neck.

.    .    .

"Karen, do you know what you're doing?"

"We'll soon know." She said and then looked at Mark. "Stop the car."

Mark slowed the pace and stopped it at the side of the road.

"Get out," Karen ordered Hudson.

"What do you want?" Hudson asked, without panicking. He was confident that Karen didn't have it in her to do what she was doing.

"Get out." Karen kept a lid on her nerves. She had to appear composed in front of her old boss. Hudson obeyed without asking another question.

Karen opened her side of the door at the same time. The Glock was now pointing at Hudson's face.

"Strip." She ordered.

"What?" Hudson could not hide his shock. He didn't notice when Mark came up behind him and snatched his Attaché. Things suddenly started to look dangerously real for Hudson.

. . .

"Karen, I'm sorry. I'm sorry for what I did to you, said to you. I promise it won't ever happen again." Hudson shifted gears quickly.

"I don't give a two-cent shit about your apology. Strip now." Karen kept a tight lid on her anger.

Hudson felt something pressing at his back. Mark had taken out his gun now.

"Don't do anything rash. I'll do what you want." Hudson said, while unbuttoning his overcoat.

Five minutes later, he was in his undergarments and shoes, shivering.

"Those as well."

"I can't."

Mark shot a bullet near his right foot, making Hudson jump.

"What the…"

.  .  .

"The next one will be in your leg." Karen said.

Hudson had no other option than to follow her orders.

"Put your hands behind your back." Karen fired another order. Hudson obeyed, and Mark quickly handcuffed him. The cold steel rubbed against his loose skin.

"Move." Mark pushed him from behind. Hudson stumbled forward.

Karen opened the boot. She grabbed Hudson's neck and pushed him inside. Her Glock was still pointed at Hudson's face. Mark swiftly tied his legs, and put a duct tape over his mouth, gagging him. Karen looked at him one last time and then shut the boot on his face.

"Now what?" Mark asked.

"We need to burn his belongings," Karen said.

"Okay," Mark said. Karen walked towards Hudson's clothes, lying on the road. Suddenly, something pierced her neck's tender skin. Before she could do anything, she was in Mark's arms and he was putting her in the back seat. She wanted to retaliate, but couldn't.

·   ·   ·

Mark tied her hands and legs. Once sure that she could not move, he grabbed Hudson's belongings and threw them in the front seat.

# CHAPTER 15

A white light blinded Karen, and she covered her face. Slug-gishly, she started to see things around her. It was a small room with a high ceiling. A nurse was checking her vitals and making notes, oblivious that her patient was awake. The bed creaked as Karen tried to move, alerting the nurse. She pressed a small blue button on the wall. Karen tried to get up. The nurse saw her struggle and moved forward to help her.

"Hello, Karen." The voice echoed in the room.

"What is this place? Where is Hudson?"

"You can leave." The voice ordered. The nurse looked at Karen and then left the room. It was now only Karen and the voice.

"This is our medical facility. You have just gone through a

medical checkup. Hudson is at a safe location."

"Why is he still alive? You and Mark betrayed me. You went back on your promise." Karen was yelling.

"Karen, I'll say this only once so listen carefully. When we helped you, we put Mark, one of our best assets, on the field for your personal mission. His face has now been seen by Hudson, along with yours. If you think we'll allow you to kill him, then you're wrong. Think what will that do to you and this team? We fight for this country, not with our own citizens. We helped you nab Hudson, but we cannot allow you to kill him. That was never part of the deal. If you still want to believe that anyone here has betrayed you, then it's your view. Also, by signing that document, you became a part of this organization and we don't let our people become their own enemy. So, if you are done with your personal problems, then tell me. We have a lot of ground to cover before we start your training."

Karen said nothing. This was not the closure she had wanted and hoped for.

"What next?" She asked, after a lot of deliberation. She didn't have an option other than to survive here. If they kicked her out because of her personal vendetta, then her next stop would probably be a prison cell.

"The next thing is to kill Karen." This grabbed Karen's attention.

.  .  .

"On the table, you will find a computer. An email from your account is sent, to the people who knew you or are related to you, stating your disappointment in the judicial system and the department. Owing to the pressure, you decided to kill yourself."

"What? I didn't send any such email."

"We did."

"But why?"

"We needed to give you an out from the system so that no one comes looking for you when you disappear."

Karen said nothing. What had she gotten herself into?

"Last night, when you were with Mark, a fire erupted in your house. Police are still looking for the reason, but they will find that you used a blowtorch to start the fire."

"What about the body?"

"They will find a body. Similar to you, but badly burnt. Unrecognizable."

· · ·

"What about the DNA?"

"That's taken care of."

"Dental records?"

"You don't need to worry about that." The voice said, "All you need to worry about is your new identity—Jessica Foster."

"Jessica?"

"The packet on the table has your passport, social security number, and a brief bio on Jessica's back story."

Karen got up from the bed and walked to the table. From the packet, she took out her passport and opened it. The name was Jessica Foster, but the photo was·not hers. It was someone else who looked oddly familiar.

"This is not my photo."

"It is you, after a small plastic surgery."

"Plastic surgery?"

.  .  .

"Yes, it will be done only if you succeed in the training. You will get these documents then. Just take the brief file on your new backstory. You'll only respond to Jessica from now. Understood?"

Karen nodded.

"You can leave the package here. Outside, you will find the nurse who was here when you woke up. She will take you to your next stop. Questions?"

"Who are you?"

"All the best, Jessica." Karen looked at the camera and gave it a blank stare.

Was she doing the right thing? Where would all this take her?

The thing that bothered her most was that her control over her life had now diminished to zero. But the time to think about it was long over. She had no option but to wait and watch how this would unfold.

*The End*

\* \* \*

# DEADLY FORCE

TASK FORCE THRILLER #2

## ABOUT DEADLY FORCE

**Sam Wick's new mission was simple - Infiltrate Iran, find the target and get out. Nothing could have gone wrong, except everything that could go wrong, went wrong.**

**Sam Wick's most explosive thriller, yet.**

**Sam Wick.** *Task Force 77's best. Master Extractor. Perfect Assassin. Task Force-77 (TF-77) is a black ops team of NSA and the US Military. This is the team, the U.S. government calls when it needs to get people out of the most dangerous places on earth.*

*For fans of Vince Flynn and Lee Child, a heart-pumping thriller of action, betrayal, split-second decisions and conspiracy by the Breakthrough Author Chase Austin.*

*What Readers are saying about Sam Wick's Adventures;*

★★★★★ *"One heck of an entertaining and intense ride... Fast, entertaining, suspenseful and action-packed... you will find your-*

*self flying through and it will be hard to let it go!" - Amazon Review*

★★★★★ *"Fast paced read with a Kick-Ass hero you can't help rooting for." - Amazon Review*

★★★★★ *"Full of awesome action. I can't wait to read the next book" - Amazon Review*

★★★★★ *" I did not put this book down for any reason other than to eat." - Amazon Review*

★★★★★ *"Fast paced, lots of thrills. Highly entertaining." - Amazon Review*

★★★★★ *"I'm ready for Sam's next assignment." - Amazon Review*

# CHAPTER 1

Dawn was just breaking, and sleepy street dogs were beginning to stir when Sam Wick completed his customary five-mile morning run. This was his third consecutive day in Tehran, the capital city of Iran, but he had been in the country in the past. He knew the place well, having spent a year or so here over the course of three previous missions. Apart from his usual run, he preferred to stay in the safe house the entire day, thinking, planning and honing the nuts and bolts of the plan. He needed the jog to take the edge off all the coffee he consumed during the day.

He checked his satellite phone—his communication line routed directly to the office of William Helms, Director of the NSA and Joint Custodian of Task Force-77, in Maryland, USA. The voice-secure sat phone was Wick's only direct link to Helms. No one else knew he was in Iran, and no one could. The administration would want complete deniability when the target was captured, even more so if anything went awry.

The safehouse was Task Force-77's property. Task Force-77, or TF-77, was a black ops team jointly overseen by the NSA and the US Army—an off-the-books team that came into play when diplomatic solutions failed. Powered with US military might across the globe and NSA's intel, the team was sent on the toughest missions in the most dangerous locations that required the use of means that no government could ever authorize officially. Its multiple assets were spread in sensitive locations across the globe, and Wick was one of the best assets TF-77 had ever produced. He was invariably chosen to undertake the riskiest exfiltration missions, especially in countries where the US could not intervene directly. Countries like Iran.

5'11". Weather-beaten face. Black hair. Pointed nose. Medium build. Unreadable sea-blue eyes and an unassuming walk. Trained in Krav Maga, Kalarippayattu and Muay Thai fighting styles. Expert in disguise. He'd been born in Kansas, but he could speak and write seventeen languages.

For anyone looking at him closely, he appeared a mass of contradictions. There was subsurface violence, almost always in control, but very much alive. There was also a pensiveness that seemed to stem from pain, yet he rarely gave vent to the anger that pain usually provoked.

Back in the safe house, he waited for the on-ground support team to arrive. To support field operatives during their missions the TF-77 deployed small on-the-ground teams—typically three to four members, depending on mission specifics. Although Wick had mentioned that he didn't need one for this mission, his bosses insisted that he take one as backup.

Wick had received a message on the TF-77 application on his cell phone. Olivia, Logan and Elijah—his support team—were on their way from Isfahan, a city in central Iran. Based on their travel plans, Wick expected them to reach the safe house in the next few hours.

This was Wick's first mission with this team. He had read their files, and they appeared competent. That's all he needed. Olivia would help him handle the logistics if required. The bonus was that she was an expert in a gunfight. Elijah was a former marine with tight credentials. Logan was a tech guy and a non-combatant. Wick had plans for each of them. If they were here, then he was fine to use them as he deemed fit in the overall mix. He had that authority. He knew that. They understood that.

He looked at his unique shopping list lying on the table. He knew where he would find the items. He had contacts in the city to get the things he needed. He grabbed his kurta to get ready. He had to get the items on his list and be back in the safe house before the support team arrived.

# CHAPTER 2

On that sunny morning, the air was heavy. The azan echoed from the loudspeakers perched at the top of the watchtower at the market square of one of the city's busiest markets.

Amid all this, Wick moved with purpose. An oversized long kurta, blue rugged jeans, black unkempt hair, and rectangular blue reading glasses gave him the look of a university student. He didn't need a false wig or eyebrows or beard to blend in with the locals. His blue eyes were the only thing that made him stand out in a place like this, and he was wearing brown contacts to hide them. Wick was aware that his physical characteristics were part of the reason that time and again he was chosen for such missions, but the more important factor was his ability to hit his targets fast and hard. Spending too long planning meant delays, and delays killed momentum. He hated that. His bosses hated that.

.  .  .

In the field, he had the final say. But he knew this power came with a lot of responsibility. One wrong decision could easily jeopardize America's image and future actions. His strategy was to minimize the factors of coincidence and luck in his missions, and the best way to do that was to do away with unnecessary antics. Keep things simple and uncomplicated. That was easier said than done in high-voltage missions like this which involved so many moving pieces. It had been a long road for him, with lots of ups and downs, to get to this stage where he now had the temperament to focus on just one thing and find the best way to get it without complications. His consistency had earned him the nickname 'the machine' from other TF-77 agents. Not that he knew or cared about such things. He was a loner and rarely spoke with anyone within the agency. There was no one in the world he could truly call his own. It was a tough way to live, but the only way he knew.

* * *

Wick walked through the throngs, his eyes carefully soaking in every small detail of his vicinity. His walk was assured yet unpretentious.

He stopped at a nondescript phone booth shop with a signboard that quite unnecessarily announced: "Phone calls". In the age of cell phones, time seemed to have stood still for paid phone booths like this. People walked past, ignoring the run-down structure and its middle-aged owner. For them, neither existed in this modern world.

Wick was probably the only customer the shop owner had seen in days, maybe even months. Wick asked if he could make a call. The man looked at him and demanded, "You have the money?"

Wick produced a torn piece of a one toman note. The owner glanced at the note, then back at Wick. Then, he reached into his desk drawer, drew out another torn note and laid it down beside the one Wick had produced. The two pieces fit together perfectly. It was an old-school way to determine authenticity in this trade and even in the age of hi-tech gizmos, it still worked like a charm. The shop owner looked at Wick and inclined his head slightly, gesturing for him to go inside.

Wick walked past the man and entered the cramped corridor behind a ragged curtain. A zero-watt bulb dangled before a door at the end of the corridor, dimly illuminating the corridor. Wick paused at the door. It was unlatched. He pushed it open and light spilled out from within. The room was separated into two sections with a long table in the middle. A young man stood on the other side holding a cell phone in his left hand. The shop owner from outside had evidently already informed him about the visitor. As soon as he saw Wick, he pulled a large black canvas bag from the floor and set it down on the table. Wick looked at the boy for a fleeting second and then, without a word, unzipped the bag and made a cursory inspection of its contents. Satisfied, he zipped the bag and lifted it. The weight seemed right too. He drew an envelope from his back pocket and slid it towards the boy. The boy counted the notes within, smiling when he saw the amount was more than that asked. Wick didn't return the smile. He backed out, without breaking eye contact with the boy. Stepping out of the room, he closed the door and crossed the corridor. In less than thirty seconds, he had left the shop and disappeared into the crowd.

# CHAPTER 3

Wick had taken utmost care in traveling to the shop, choosing secluded alleyways and inner streets. Still, the whole business deal had taken less than three hours and he was back in the safe house well in time.

Putting the bag down in the dining area, he checked his watch. In a few hours he would be dropped off as close to the target as they could manage. From there he would be on his own.

He had everything laid out and, for the next half hour, he meticulously analyzed the contents of the bag. This routine, which he followed without fail on every mission, ensured no mistakes. It meant that he would not head into war territory only to find his gun jammed, or his ammunition low, or any of the other thousand possibilities that could occur in the heat of combat. He was always coming up with ways to be more efficient on the battlefield. This line of thinking explained the arsenal he chose for his missions. Operatives of his caliber—of which there were few—

often spent hours selecting tailor-made, customized weapons. Not Wick.

He saw nothing but potential problems in guns like that. Most of them were largely untested. He had faced that problem first-hand, ceding control due to a gun malfunctioning during combat and paying dearly for it. He now preferred the toughest, most steadfast arsenal for himself. The weapons that would never in a million years jam on the battlefield.

Over the next thirty minutes, he disassembled all his weapons and checked each part for flaws with extreme patience and care. There was a time for brashness and recklessness, but it wasn't before the mission began.

Olivia entered the safe house when Wick was in the process of re-assembling the guns. Behind her came Logan and Elijah. They nodded at each other and set about their respective tasks with robotic precision.

Ten minutes later, Wick was standing at the right side of the center table with them. Olivia was going over each detail. They had done this already by video conference but doing it in person was critical. The team was very thorough in this regard. They had planned a concise tactical operation order, breaking down the mission to the last detail. Wick's experience of working with the Special Forces teams told him that this team had been with one of the military's elite units.

. . .

"We will be out in forty minutes," Wick stated at the end of the recap.

Then began the standard operating procedure. Before leaving the safe house, all notes had to be burnt. Radio frequencies, escape routes, maps, passwords, codes — everything was committed to memory. Everyone's fake credentials were placed in flash bags. If things went wrong, all they had to do was pull a string on the bag and its contents would be incinerated instantly.

Everything had been planned and rehearsed multiple times, but Wick didn't have a good feeling about this one. He couldn't quite put his finger on the reason for his unease.

He was reminded of a mission, early in his career, where he had been confident about everything and, by the end of it, more than twenty US soldiers were dead. Ever since then, he had never really felt completely confident about any mission. Still, this feeling was different. Was he losing his edge? Maybe. He was just twenty-seven but over the last few years he had been consistently running head-on into dangerous situations and somehow getting out of them alive; and every time something within him changed.

He had been an angry man for so many years and had always used that anger to sharpen his focus, but now the fury was mellowing. He knew that sooner or later this lost intensity would cost him his life. Luckily, he had had no woman in his life so far; flings, but nothing serious. However, that stance was also changing. Now he wanted to feel something different — maybe something on the opposite pole of hatred. Maybe he wanted to put his life as a TF-77 operative behind him and move on. Maybe.

Elijah removed his headphones and announced, "The first set of guests to the convention have arrived."

Wick checked his watch. It was twenty minutes to one, about ninety minutes before the strike. It was time to check with Helms one more time. Wick grabbed the COMSAT mobile phone and carried it to the next room.

# CHAPTER 4

MARYLAND, USA

If William Helms had bothered to look outside the large glass window in his office, he would have seen a white-faced Storm-Petrel sitting on the windowsill outside. Unfortunately, times and tides were both working against the USA leaving no space for stopping to admire life's little pleasures. The weak leadership in Washington and an inconsistent foreign policy had left America on shaky ground—under attack both externally and internally. Russia, China, Iran—all were closing in for the kill.

The fifty-eight-year-old director wasn't one to be interested in petty Washington politics, but the current situation demanded that he think politically while dispatching his primary responsibility—protecting his motherland.

Personally, he had always kept Washington at an arm's distance.

The town loved drama and politicians loved overacting. Despite multiple warnings in the past, they had all downplayed the foreign threats as temporary blips in the overall picture, but Helms knew that these temporary blips could soon turn into painful scars if not checked in time. He had never let his guard down, even for a minute. He knew no one on Capitol Hill liked him. Many respected him but they all hated his guts. He had no friends here.

Helms was at the top of the intelligence food chain. Every piece of information in the world went through the NSA's fine net. The agency combed through an unimaginable quantity of e-mails, internet phone calls, photos, videos, file transfers, and social networking data from big internet companies, including Google, Facebook, Apple, Amazon, YouTube, Skype, and Microsoft, besides WeChat, Sina Weibo and Tencent QQ from China; and Paltalk, a video-chat service popular in the Middle East and among Muslims.

No one knew exactly how much Helms knew, and no one wanted to find out. Rumor had it that he already had thick dossiers on everyone who mattered on the global political stage, including the who's who of Washington.

Helms knew that the politicians couldn't imagine possessing such valuable information and not using it, but his entire career was built upon only one premise—keeping secrets secret. He also knew that this was of no comfort to those sitting in Washington with a checkered past.

.   .   .

He was pained by the changing political scenarios, but his immediate focus was the job at hand. The team in Tehran had been given the go-ahead by POTUS (President of The United States) to extract a civilian. And not just any civilian. Helms stared at the eight-by-twelve black-and-white photograph clipped to the dossier on his desk. The man was known as Majeed el-Abdullah, an Iranian cleric and an important figurehead of the Shi'a population. The president took a lot of convincing to authorize the extraction of someone like him, who not only was a civilian but also a religious figurehead of one of America's fiercest rivals. Before 1980, Iran had been one of the United States' closest allies. But after the 1979 Revolution, which ousted the pro-American Shah and replaced him with the anti-American Supreme Leader Ayatollah Ruhollah Khomeini, things had changed quickly. The developments even surprised the United States government, its State Department and intelligence services, who consistently underestimated the magnitude and long-term implications of this unrest. Six months before the revolution culminated, the CIA had produced a report stating that "Iran is not in a revolutionary or even a 'prerevolutionary' situation." Clearly, they had badly misread the situation. In any case, Iran and the United States had had no formal diplomatic relations since 1980. And the Iranians were nothing if not vocal about perceived American arrogance and its desire for global dominance.

All this made the president wary of the backlash if the mission went kaput. He was already on shaky ground and something like this could end his presidency in a snap. His only reason to agree to this mission was Helms. Helms had convinced him to go ahead with this, Helms was shouldering a lot of responsibility, and that's why his only choice was Sam Wick, a man he could trust with his own life.

.   .   .

The cleric had first landed on the NSA's radar five years back when the NSA was tracking Al Qaeda's money trail through Russia and Germany. The information received was deadly. Al Qaeda was planning to build chemical weapons, and the cleric was the face behind getting the money for it. The location was in Iran, near the Iran-Afghanistan border. Just before production started the US president threatened the Iranian leadership with airstrikes and more sanctions. Iran eventually closed the facility, and the cleric decided to search for a new place to fulfill his mission.

Five years later the USA once again discovered the site of the new weapons plant. Al Qaeda was almost on the verge of completing a new plant deep below a mountain. This time it required much more force and time was not on America's side. The cleric was leading the mission once again, and he had made sure that only a nuclear strike could destroy the facility.

A nuclear attack meant inviting a war when the USA was least ready to engage in one. The only other way was to extract the cleric to the US military base in Pakistan which shared a border with Iran and then track his aides one by one. Getting him alive was key to the whole operation, and Wick was the best extractor TF-77 had ever created.

Helms flipped through the dossier, looking at a series of photos and translated conversations that the cleric had had with Al Qaeda operatives. This relationship concerned the NSA most. Helms knew that there would be only one target for the weapons they were creating—the US.

.   .   .

On the next page were photos of the cleric convention that was scheduled to take place later that day. This was where the cleric was most exposed and would be at his most vulnerable.

NSA analysts had crunched tons and tons of data to find the relevant bits to aid the team. If all went as planned, Helms expected to have the cleric in their custody in the next few hours.

# CHAPTER 5

Helms' secure line phone rang, and he picked up before the second ring.

"We are ready to go," Wick's voice echoed through the speaker.

"Updates?"

Wick ran down the checklist of developments and explained the final touches he had added to the plan with Olivia and the team. Helms heard him out with rapt attention. He asked no questions.

When Wick was done, he said, "This is our only chance. If you miss him today, I doubt we'll get another one. The cat will be out of the bag and there'll I be too many eyes on us for another attempt."

.   .   .

"I understand," Wick said.

He didn't sound like his confident self and Helms picked up the slight variation in his tone.

"Is there anything else?" he asked in a mellower tone. Wick was more than his best asset; Helms had seen him transform from a naïve boy to an efficient assassin.

"Everything's fine," Wick responded.

There was a moment of silence, then Helms asked, "What's your gut telling you on this one?"

Wick didn't know what to make of this question. He hadn't discussed his personal feelings with anyone in a very long time, and this was his boss, Helms, on the other side of the line. Should he let him know about the unease he was feeling?

Wick's forehead was moist. He was calling from the bathroom, which was cramped, with little or no ventilation. He gripped the handset, not sure if Helms was just asking for the sake of asking or if he genuinely wanted to know. He didn't share a very close relationship with him. Finally, he said, "I'm sure it's nothing. Just the usual anxiety before we hit the target. A little more prep time would have been nice, but that's usually the case."

.   .   .

"If there's something not right, don't force it," Helms said again.

"I can handle this." Wick hated himself for exposing his slight moment of self-doubt.

"I'm not going to second-guess you if you don't want to do it."

"That's never been the case. I don't care about what others think of my methods, and nobody knows that better than you." Wick smiled quietly.

Helms knew what he was talking about. Wick's tendency to keep to himself was often seen as arrogance in the agency. The other thing that irked people was his nature to call a spade a spade. Wick said it like it was and never shied away from telling the truth, even in front of the president. Once, In the past administration, Helms had taken him to a briefing. He hadn't wanted to, but Wick had been the most knowledgeable person around about the man they were going to discuss. The meeting had gone smoothly as long as Wick wasn't speaking but once he discerned that they were going ahead with the worst plan of his entire career, there had been no stopping him. He had told the president to his face that if he was going to go ahead with that plan, he might as well send his men with suicide bomber jackets or a cyanide pill because the plan was as good as his morning dump. Wick hadn't even waited for the president to throw him out of the meeting. He had seen himself out as soon as he was done massacring the plan of action. The president had been furious and had gone ahead with the plan anyway, but the results were exactly what Wick had predicted. Fewer men would have been killed on a suicide mission than on that particular job.

"You know what I mean. Just be careful." Helms was concerned.

"I always am." Wick was now answering without thinking.

"Anything else?" asked Helms.

"Nope."

"All right ... good luck, and keep me in the loop."

"Okay." Wick ended the call. Opening the bathroom door, he stepped out. He still couldn't shake that feeling deep in his stomach. Something wasn't right.

# CHAPTER 6

Wick put the finishing touches on his disguise. A rinse dye had turned his black hair grayish white. Special contacts transformed his eyes to mild brown, and the makeup made his complexion more wheatish. Wick checked the clothes on the bed and checked his equipment one last time.

The oversized kurta had hidden compartments that were loaded with weapons from his laundry list. The shoes he was going to wear looked broken and old, but they contained his fake Iranian and American passports and twenty grand in cash in Iranian currency. The Iranian passport had Wick's photo, an alias, and stamps indicating that he had entered the country through Turkmenistan. The American passport contained a photograph of Wick with a trimmed beard and short hair. They were his way out of Iran if something went wrong. No one, not even the folks in

Maryland, knew about them. If things fell apart, Wick wanted to be able to go completely off-radar.

Wick had already memorized the main streets, alleyways, nearest bus stations and railway routes that would get him out of the area if his pickup failed. He carried a minuscule GPS tracker in his watch to make sure he always knew his exact location. A matte-black K-Bar was concealed in the right sleeve of the kurta, and four extra clips of 9-mm rounds were hidden in various parts of his clothes. Wick's earpiece would keep him in touch with his team, who would wait for him in a rusty stolen minivan outside the convention center. The minivan had been repainted and given a nondescript trademark along with Iran's national emblem in red.

He was going into the mission with his trusty 9-mm Glock-26 pistol. The serial number had been removed. The clip had fifteen rounds, and with four more clips, Wick had enough for a small battle. This was his backup, although he planned to get the job done without firing a single bullet. Before leaving the room, he wiped the surfaces to remove any trace of fingerprints. When he walked into the other room Olivia, Logan and Elijah were doing the same. When they were finished, they looked at Wick, who gestured for them to strap the three bulletproof vests below their oversized attires.

A few moments later they left the safe house and got into the van. Olivia was behind the wheel and Elijah was in the passenger seat. Wick and Logan were at the back. The minivan rolled gently down the rutted dirt road.

# CHAPTER 7

The drive to their destination would take about forty minutes. Wick and Logan studied the landscape from their respective windows. Wick moved and his eyes suddenly fell on his reflection in the dusty, cracked, rear-view mirror of the stolen minivan. He wondered how long it had been since he had lived with his real face. He was camouflaged as a beggar. His eyes betrayed the lack of sleep that was normal for him before every mission.

There was still some time before his drop. Wick scanned the thin file in his hand once again. He had already committed it to memory, but he had nothing else to do for the next fifteen minutes. Reading the file again seemed as good a way as any to pass the time.

He turned over the first page and looked at the bold headline: Iran's Minister of Culture and Islamic Guidance, Heyder Mohammad Najjar, says a meeting of clerics will convene in Tehran on 29th November for promoting religious harmony.

.  .  .

Clerics from the United Arab Emirates, Pakistan, Saudi Arabia, Myanmar, Syria, Iraq and Turkey had been invited to the convention. Tehran's Mayor, Fazlollah Golshaeeyan, would host the convention along with Minister Heyder Mohammad Najjar. This was where their target would arrive.

With the change in the US administration, the sanctions on Iran had been re-imposed. Other nations, fearful of angering the US government, had started distancing themselves from the country. The leadership of Iran feared that if the situation continued to deteriorate, the temporary alienation could soon be a damning reality. The country was getting cornered on the world stage and needed a shot in the arm to re-enter the fold of its brethren. Iran's Supreme Leader had given Heyder Mohammad Najjar the responsibility for regaining the support of other Muslim nations. This cleric convention was the first step in that direction.

Wick went back to the first page that showed a picture of his target for this mission—Majeed el-Abdullah. The man in the picture wore specs and had a long, snowy beard. His eyes looked cold and calculating. He had been the head of Iran's hardline judiciary for the decade from 2001 to 2011, during which he had carried out more than two thousand executions, including four adolescents, despite Iran having signed the UN Convention on the Rights of the Child, which prohibited such killings. He had also allowed the arbitrary arrests of political and human-rights activists, the torture of prisoners, and the closure of reformist newspapers that supposedly tarnished Iran's image.

.  .  .

Recently, Iran's Supreme Leader had appointed Majeed Head of the Expediency Council, a body intended to resolve disputes between parliament and a watchdog body, the Guardian Council.

Majeed had been born in the city of Najaf in Iraq to Iranian parents. In the 1970s he had been jailed and tortured by Saddam Hussein's security forces because of his political activities. He had moved to Iran after the Islamic revolution in 1979 and risen rapidly through the ranks. In recent years, Majeed had aimed to raise his profile in Iraq as a replacement for the top Shi'ite cleric.

He had, time and again, given statements to the effect that Iran had been created to conquer the Christians as per the prophecy made in Hadith.

"Iranians should consider themselves fortunate that Allah has bestowed on them the honor of waging war against evil forces like the US," Majeed was recorded saying recently in a rally attended by more than 50,000 people.

In the same rally, Majeed had also claimed that the Prophet had predicted there would be a war soon, and Iran was destined to win and rule its neighbors and the western countries. "The genesis of Iran was prophesied to defeat the evil forces of Christianity," he had declared.

But Wick knew that behind this facade of a religious fanatic lay a keen brain that was plotting the fall of America through chemical warfare.

# CHAPTER 8

Majeed descended the stairs into a small bunker on the outskirts of Tehran. He had fifty minutes before he had to leave for the convention.

The bunker was one of many built by a terrorist group that acted as a front for Al-Qaeda in Iran. Public perception was that Al-Qaeda regarded Shia Muslims as heretics and attacked their mosques and gatherings, and the group had been designated a terrorist organization by Iran. However, Al-Qaeda and Iran had allied during the 1990s when Hezbollah had trained Al-Qaeda operatives. Iran had detained hundreds of Al-Qaeda operatives who entered the country following the 2001 invasion of Afghanistan. Even though the Iranian government had held most of them under house arrest, limited their freedom of movement, and closely monitored their activities, the U.S. had expressed concerns that Iran had not fully accounted for their whereabouts, culminating in accusations of Iranian complicity in the 2003 Riyadh compound bombings.

·   ·   ·

The terrorist group that acted as a front for Al-Qaeda was formed in December 2010, when about eighteen groups had united under the leadership of Baitullah Maksud. Its objectives were resistance against the western states, enforcement of their interpretation of sharia, and a plan to unite against NATO-led forces in Iraq.

Baitullah Maksud was a ghost; no one knew what he looked like. The CIA had tried hard, but they had not been able to find a recent photo of him. All they had in their files was an old, hazy image of Maksud which had hitherto proved useless in their attempts to trace him.

Once Maksud and his men deserted the bunker, others had tried briefly to take it over, but they soon had to abandon it and run for their lives. Since then it had remained desolate, until Majeed took over the fields that Maksud had once owned.

Outside the bunker, an army of militants sporting AK-47s secured the area. Inside the dark cellar, Majeed and his trusted aide Abdul Farhad approached the two steel chairs in which two badly bruised semi-conscious bodies were tied—US army officers.

"Your government is very stubborn. We asked them to comply with our demands and yet they are dawdling. No respect for your sacrifice. I feel sad for you and your families." Majeed threw a copy of the Washington Post on the floor. "Look at the headlines, they are talking about Russia and China. They are busy twiddling their thumbs. They have already forgotten about you."

. . .

There was no response.

Majeed looked at Farhad. Majeed was still reeling from the setback he had had to face a few years ago, and he knew that since then America had never left him alone. It also meant that the new underground facility he was building beneath a mountain could be under surveillance.

Yet there wasn't any warning. Maybe they were waiting for the right time. What could be the right time?

If he were in their shoes, he would plan a strike near D-Day.

Once he understood the dynamics, he had accelerated his plans. His understanding had opened up new options for him. Being a religious leader, he knew that his position was secure, but the facility had no such veil of safety. The compressed timelines meant moving the D-Day forward. This time he was ready for any surprise. Because this time he would not fail to deliver.

His team had grabbed two US military officers a few weeks ago to keep DC off guard. He had planned their deaths today. The backlash would allow him some breathing space while the whole world watched and condemned the murder of two US soldiers.

# CHAPTER 9

Majeed picked up the copies of the Washington Post and shoved them into the torn military uniforms of the two soldiers.

He asked Farhad to get the mission files. The dossiers were a product of months of tedious and meticulous work. Each file represented hours and hours of surveillance notes, in-depth subject profiles, and maps of chosen neighborhoods throughout the D.C. metropolitan area. He wasn't going to bomb the whole city. Instead, Majeed had chosen his targets carefully—the who's who of DC, and of the White House.

Majeed and his select mercenaries knew when the police patrolled the designated areas, when the newspapers were delivered, who jogged at what time, and most importantly: where their targets slept and what time they awoke. He and his men had stalked them for months, watching and waiting, patiently discerning which part of their daily routine could be exploited and when they would be most vulnerable. In the next four days, his men would start their mission to decimate the Americans on their soil. The time, places and targets had all been chosen. In less than a week, the course of America would be changed forever. Every minute detail was now stored in a USB flash drive hanging from a gold chain around his neck.

Stuffing the files along with the newspapers into his prisoners' clothes, Majeed turned to Farhad. "Burn them when I reach the convention center."

# CHAPTER 10

The minivan had stopped in an alleyway, some two miles from the convention center. First, Olivia and Elijah left the minivan to scope out the scene. Not a single person in sight. They opened the back door of the minivan and Wick stepped out.

Inside the van, Logan sat with his eyes glued to small laptop screens, his earpieces in place. The team had clear orders from the TF-77 command center. They needed Majeed alive at any cost. There was no room for error, and that's why they had Wick on the mission.

As Wick walked away from the minivan, Logan decided to check the comms one more time.

"Wick, can you hear me?"

.   .   .

"Crystal. Over." Wick checked his watch. He still had four hours before darkness set in.

* * *

He had to cover the remaining two miles on foot. He already had the security details of the convention center imprinted in his eidetic memory, but he wanted to see it firsthand.

Walking down the busy Tehran street meant leaving a lot of eyewitnesses for the police, but no one looked at Wick twice. The disguise was impeccable. The dirty, grey, unkempt beard, and a white headscarf rubbed with scum and now almost greyish black, hid his features. His clothes smelled as if he had shared a sty with a bunch of pigs. Most people refused to acknowledge his existence. The smell ensured they kept their distance. They never looked at the two mildly brown eyes on a face which, when cleaned and shaved and bathed, would be the most good-looking one on the whole street. For them, he was just another beggar, a normal sight on the city streets, a sight to be ignored.

Wick walked towards the convention center, not too slow, not too fast, just the right shuffle of a person who was hungry and had difficulty walking.

Three hundred yards from the convention center, the security started to thicken. Local uniforms crowded the area, deployed for security. The tight security cover was unusual for a religious convention, but he saw a few beggars loitering near the convention center. The sight gave him some hope.

．　．　．

Wick saw two policemen on duty, standing and talking to each other at the corner of the sharp turn that led to the convention center.

"Hundred yards away from the convention center. Over," he whispered in the earpiece plugged in his ear, hidden by the headscarf. He kept walking.

One of the two policemen glanced casually in his direction and then went back to his conversation.

"Everyone ready?"

The acknowledgements on the receiver assured him they could hear him. Everything was on track. He maintained a steady pace towards the policemen.

As he neared them, both men turned to look at him, wrinkling their noses at the smell. Wick didn't pause or stop.

"Disgusting, how can anyone be so filthy?" one of the police officers commented to the other.

"Shoo, shoo." The other gestured with his hand for Wick to keep away, but Wick kept his head down and pretended not to hear.

The distance was reducing. Soon both uniforms wanted nothing more than for the smell to go away. With one hand covering their mouths and noses, they started to yell at Wick. Wick continued to approach them, throwing his arms in the air, making a gagging sound like a retard.

They had to make a decision soon. The stench was unbearable. One of the two policemen raised his baton at Wick, who made an unsure gesture with his hands to block the incoming blow.

"Shoo!" his colleague yelled thinking Wick would bolt out of the fear of getting beaten up, but Wick wasn't going to back out so easily. In his attempt to save himself, he knowingly tripped and fell on the ground, making wild howling noises. The moving baton hit his right arm but couldn't connect properly due to Wick's fall. The policeman raised the baton again but a man's voice from behind made him pause.

"Hashem, what the hell?" Both policemen whirled around and straightened perceptibly; the voice obviously belonged to their superior. "The caravan is arriving, why is that side of the street still not cleared?"

The policemen forgot all about Wick as they rushed to clear the part of the street that had attracted their superior's ire. Wick quickly got up and started to walk.

Wick turned the corner and continued to shuffle on. He didn't turn around to see what the two uniforms were doing behind his back, but he could imagine them directing the pedestrians and cars to clear the street.

The turn opened into a new street that had more uniforms patrolling on both sides. A few of them glanced at him casually but no one paid much heed. They were busy with their superiors shouting orders at them to keep the streets clear.

"Target is arriving from the north. Over." Wick's earpiece crackled.

"Copy. Over."

He stopped and turned towards the cavalcade's entry point in the north. There was a whirring sound of rubber on gravel and seconds later an entourage of three white Toyota Fortuners came down the street, headed for the convention center's elevated entrance. The SUVs slowed at the stairs leading to the large gate of the center. As soon as the vehicles came to a halt, the minister and the mayor came hurrying down the stairs to welcome their guest of honor for the event. Ten gunmen rapidly got out of the first and third SUV and rushed towards the vehicle in the middle. The left side passenger seat door opened and Majeed leisurely stepped out.

"As-salāmu Alaykum," Majeed greeted the minister and the mayor.

.   .   .

"Alaykum as-salām Janab,'" they replied in unison. 'We are glad that you are finally here. Hope the journey was peaceful.'

"Insha Allah, it was good, except for the traffic." He smiled.

Wick studied Majeed and his security detail from across the street. Majeed looked older than in the photo. But there was no doubt it was him. His target was finally here. A few feet away from him.

Wick decided to linger at the same spot till the uniforms let him be. He had already earmarked a few places near the center where he might head if he was shooed away from here. Now he had to wait till the convention ended. Another seventy-five minutes or so.

&ast; &ast; &ast;

Once settled, Wick started to scope the area carefully. On the ground, the center was surrounded by uniforms, no snipers though. Wick had checked with Logan, too. No communication intercepted about any snipers. Still, for a religious convention, the security detail was unusual.

Remaining where he was, he glanced at the predetermined exit routes. The alleyway left of the building was secured by three uniforms. They could be an issue, but if the plan went perfectly, he wouldn't have to worry about them.

. . .

His eyes swept the street from left to right to see if anything could derail the plan.

The guests had arrived, and the convention had probably started. Traffic started to drip onto the street again.

Wick sat in a nondescript spot on the footpath, head down. He took a stale piece of bread from his inner pocket and started to chew on it. If another uniform demanded to know what he was doing there, he could always point to the bread and begin a long, woeful story that would hopefully see him through the situation. No one did. Wick's focus was on the large entrance of the convention center to his right and the exit road to his extreme left.

It didn't take long for traffic on the street to return to its chaotic norm. Pedestrians and cyclists made it worse. A sedan took the wrong lane and brought the entire traffic to a standstill. One of the uniforms, who looked like a higher-ranking officer, yelled at two of his underlings to clear the mess.

The two uniforms grudgingly left their positions to take up traffic duty.

Wick's habit of continually scanning his surrounding area was in overdrive. His instincts checked for any anomaly on the crowded street. And then he thought he saw something.

. . .

A seven or eight-year-old boy was walking on the opposite pavement. He looked sad, with eyes swollen from crying.

After standing at attention for several hours, the uniforms were relaxing till the convention was over. The two officers busy on traffic duty were closer to the boy, but their focus was on unsnarling the traffic. Amid all the loud honking, innumerable vehicles and pedestrians, no one had the time to wonder what a boy was doing alone on that street. No one except Wick.

He was trained to find anomalies in perfectly normal situations, and the lone boy was an anomaly. His wearing a jacket in the sweltering heat of Tehran under a blazing sun was an anomaly. And the swollen eyes—maybe he had been crying hard or sleeping less or maybe he was angry.

Sadness with a strong hint of visible anger was an anomaly. The slow measured walk towards the center's entrance was an anomaly.

If one looked close enough, there were signs written all over the kid that he was about to derail months of intricate planning in seconds.

But Wick was worried about one more thing. He was a child: a misled kid at the wrong place at the wrong time. He didn't know what he was doing and to whom. Anger rose inside Wick. Who would do that to an innocent? He desperately wanted to save the boy, but he could see the bulge in his jacket, which could be a bomb. The bomb could be remote-controlled or pressure-triggered, in either case, it was already a checkmate. The boy was very close to the entrance. Any move now would be a wrong move. If he tried to save the boy or tried to take him away from the location, invariably the bomb would go off. There would be hundreds of casualties.

He looked around for the person, who was bound to be somewhere close, who was keeping an eye on the child to make sure everything went as planned, to see if enough people died. For Wick, it also meant that his original timeline – to wait until the convention was over – had now gone kaput.

He instinctively whispered in the earpiece. "Abort mission. I repeat, abort mission. Activate Plan B. Over." A couple of surprised acknowledgements and the static resumed.

Wick's eyes scanned the three sides visible to him. His back was secured by a concrete wall. That was one area he could ignore to save time.

He could go directly to the alleyway where the three uniforms he had seen earlier were still standing. It would take him five minutes to get there if he walked. He knew he couldn't run. People would shoot him first and ask questions later.

He could continue to his left, but it meant more uniforms and more impact if the bomb went off.

.   .   .

That only left one option—retracing his steps and taking cover behind the concrete wall beyond the turn. He stood up and retraced his steps. Almost there. He sped up. He was at the corner and was about to turn when a powerful blow jolted him from behind. His body left the tarmac and hit a nearby car with insane force.

# CHAPTER 11

Sections of the thick concrete wall disintegrated, destroying a large part of the wall structure at the turn.

The ear-splitting blast knocked the wind out of Wick's lungs. At such a close range, he was lucky to still be breathing. Shrapnel flew everywhere. Something grazed the side of Wick's head, causing him to black out for a few seconds. When he regained his senses, the world had changed.

Pieces of debris still showered down on him. His ears were ringing. He couldn't hear a thing. It was as if the world had gone to hell. He tried getting up. A jolt of pain ran up his right arm, but his legs still seemed to be functioning.

He turned towards the convention center. Dust and smoke engulfed the street. Burnt dead bodies lay strewn on the ground. There were shadows of people, some of whom were like walking ghosts. Others moved as though in great pain, like scarecrows, their arms held out from their bodies, forearms and hands dangling. With a sudden flash of understanding, he realized that they had been burned and were holding their arms out to prevent the painful friction of raw surfaces rubbing together. Dust and the smell burning flesh filled his lungs.

When the dust finally settled, he saw that the front part of the large convention center building had been destroyed.

Then he saw Majeed being ushered by his bodyguards towards an alleyway opposite the convention center where his SUVs suddenly appeared, possibly summoned by one of his bodyguards.

Wick ignored his pain and sprinted towards the SUVs. His Glock was out, barrel pointing down. By the time he turned in the alley-way, the three vehicles were already in motion. The middle SUV's door opened and Majeed almost flew inside.

"The target is moving. Over," he shouted but there was no response. He lifted a hand to his ear. The earpiece was missing. There was no time to find it. The target was moving, and Wick had no clue where he was headed.

# CHAPTER 12

Wick followed the SUVs on foot as they maneuvered through the dead bodies and the debris. He was still disoriented and stumbled every few steps. But the ringing in his ears was mellowing down.

The SUV crossed the location where Wick had seen the boy. There was a large pool of blood where the boy had been. No body parts.

With a sense of detachment, Wick noticed severed limbs, a blood-soaked watch, flip-flops, and a pair of shoes. He did not have time to think about the devastation he had just been a part of. The three SUVs were picking up speed. He had to find his rhythm. Majeed was going to get away. Plan B wouldn't work if they didn't know where he was going.

He checked his pocket. The GPS tracking device was still there.

If he could attach it to the second SUV in line, the plan could still work. But the cavalcade was fast getting out of reach. He tried picking up his pace, but his legs were not ready for a longer sprint. The pain in his right hand was growing too. The explosion had been too close. The realization hit him that his body was in no state to chase a moving vehicle on foot, and he desperately looked around for a deserted vehicle.

He searched around, anything to take him further. A Yamaha lay on its side; there were no keys. He snapped the wires from beneath the engine and hotwired the ignition. The engine coughed twice, refusing to start. He tried once more and succeeded.

No one was looking at him. People were busy saving themselves. In a few minutes, the streets would be crowded with the bomb squad, local police, and every other government agency.

He revved the throttle. The Yamaha started slowly, then picked up speed. Maneuvering through the by lanes, he sped towards Majeed's SUV.

Wick knew that if anyone checked the rearview mirror, not only would they be alerted, but Wick would probably find a bullet heading for him.

His scummy robe flowing back in the wind messed his balance. He thought of getting rid of it but then decided against it.

.   .   .

He still didn't know how he was going to attach the GPS tracker. Between him and the rearmost Fortuner was another car shielding him from a direct line of attack.

He was focused on maintaining a steady speed when the traffic ahead of him started to slow. Two hundred yards ahead was an intersection and the signal was red. As Wick slowed his motor-cycle, a plan started to form in his head.

# CHAPTER 13

By the time the traffic came to a complete halt, Wick was already on his feet, leaving the stolen Yamaha in the middle of the road. The wind and the maneuvering had made him temporarily forget his pain. Once he was back on foot it returned, and he started stumbling again. The good thing was that his senses were back to normal, and he was able to think straight.

Perhaps because of the blast, the traffic at the red light was extremely slow. The signal was working intermittently, and a traffic policeman was manually managing the traffic.

Wick's walk changed as he neared the rearmost SUV. He sauntered as if his left leg was hurt. His hand in front of him begging for alms. The GPS tracker was in between his right index and middle finger.

He knocked on the driver's side of the windshield. The driver glanced at him and gestured impatiently for him to move on. Wick didn't knock a second time. He moved forward toward Majeed's SUV.

Majeed was in the middle row of seats surrounded by two gunmen on both sides. He knocked on the windshield and all three men looked at him with disgust. His eyes met Majeed's, and he knew that Majeed had looked through him as he would any homeless beggar. The gunman sitting on Wick's side waved him away. Wick continued to stand there, looking at the three of them, begging for alms.

The signal turned green and the first SUV started to roll. Majeed's Fortuner followed suit. This was the time. Wick remained where he was, hand held out, and as the rear side of Majeed's Fortuner neared him, he discreetly attached the GPS tracker to the steel. He stood there, watching the three SUVs moving in tandem. They had not realized what Wick had done.

*Plan B was set in motion.*

# CHAPTER 14

Wick returned to his Yamaha, which was still standing in the middle of the road, the cars behind it honking impatiently. He made an apologetic face at the nearest driver while ignoring his shocked expressions that a beggar could afford a motorcycle like that. He wheeled the Yamaha to the side of the road, allowing the traffic to pass. In the opposite lane, it looked like every vehicle in the city was speeding towards the explosion site.

Wick had no way to contact his support team. The only way to reconnect was to return to the safe house. He started the engine, pressing the accelerator to give it the required thrust, and made a turn at the next intersection. His knowledge of city streets would come in handy now that he no longer had a GPS unit. Five hundred yards later, he turned left into a deserted alley.

Twenty-seven minutes through narrow alleys eventually brought him close to the safe house. He abandoned the motorcycle three blocks away from the base and covered the rest of the way on foot. The walk didn't cause him any discomfort, and that was the good news, although his hearing was still not fully functional.

The safe house was locked, and the minivan was nowhere to be seen. He pulled the keypad coverup and keyed in the code for the day. The door slid to its left and he squeezed inside, not waiting for it to open completely.

Three seconds later the door closed behind him. Hearing the sound, Elijah came out into the hallway. Olivia was behind him.

Olivia stared at him, "Oh my god! You okay?"

He nodded and removed his robe at the door.

"We thought we lost you in the blast." Olivia sounded worried.

"I'm fine," he said it in a matter-of-fact tone and walked into the inner room, where Logan sat at a computer screen. "How strong is the GPS signal?"

"Good," Logan replied, studying the screen. "The vehicle is still in motion. The possible locations could be here and here." Logan tapped his finger on the screen.

.   .   .

One of the locations was a two-story house on the outskirts of the city, around thirty miles from the safe house.

"Bring up the images from the satellite feed," Wick said.

Logan's fingers flew over the keyboard. Meanwhile, Wick turned to Elijah and Olivia, who were still looking at him with a multitude of questions in their eyes.

"Not now, please."

Olivia nodded. "Helms asked for you," she said.

"'ll talk to him soon. In the meantime, you can relay to him that we're going ahead with the backup plan."

"Wick, there's one more thing," Elijah said.

Wick looked at him with a neutral expression.

"We just received news that the two US soldiers captured by Baitullah Maksud's terrorist group were burned to death. This was broadcast live on the Internet worldwide.

Wick registered every word. He said nothing, yet everyone in the room felt the tension rise a few notches. Wick's jaw stiffened. His eyes turned cold. His posture tensed.

"You think talking to Helms now would make sense?" Elijah asked.

"Show me the latest images of Majeed's house."

Logan complied. The images appeared on the white wall in front of them.

"What's Majeed's current position?" Wick asked. The lack of emotion in his tone surprised everyone, but no one said anything.

The image on the wall changed to show a yellow dot moving towards the house.

"Any intel on who orchestrated the blast?"

"We're circling on the suspects. The signature is similar to that of the Al-Hamas group but not completely. One of our agents is at the location, sending us intel on all the ongoing developments."

The yellow dot on the screen stopped at the house.

.  .  .

"We need to move fast now. This is our only chance to capture Majeed," Wick said looking at the image. He was pissed at the way things were shaping up. "Show me the security details of the house."

A new image showed the building surrounded by black dots— the top view of people's heads. Five in total. Two at the entry and three at the back.

The photo changed again. This one showed Majeed walking towards the house with another man, who Wick assumed was Farhad, known as 'the enforcer' in local lingo, who shadowed Majeed everywhere.

"We're leaving in thirty minutes."

He went into the other room and closed the door behind him. He needed a quick bath and some painkillers. Everyone else in the hall exchanged looks and started to kit up.

The warm water washed the scum and blood from his body, clearing his mind. He was a loner and so far, Olivia and the team had given him the wide berth he needed to be at his peak. It wasn't a privilege, but his need. It also meant that if anything went wrong, it was his head on the chopping block, but it gave him the freedom to make critical on-the-spot decisions without waiting for permissions or approvals.

.  .  .

He closed his eyes and the face of the boy appeared on the back of his eyelids. The boy's gaze drained of innocence stared back at him.

# CHAPTER 15

Twenty minutes later, when Olivia opened the door Wick was putting on his Kevlar bulletproof vest. His long, messy hair was tied neatly in a ponytail. The long beard was still there, but minus the dirt. He had ditched the loose clothes and wore a comfortable Dry-fit t-shirt. He looked clean and ready.

He walked up to the laptop and checked the GPS location of Majeed's SUV. It was still parked at the same location. The satellite had sent two more images minutes ago. The other two SUVs had not accompanied Majeed's. No change in the number of gatekeepers either, still two in the front and three at the back. The three guards at the back were busy drinking and smoking.

"Here's the plan," Wick started. "We'll stop the minivan approximately one-and-a-half miles away from the location. Elijah, Olivia and I will cover the rest of the distance on foot. Logan will guide us from the van. You both," he turned to Olivia and Elijah, "will take the three at the back and anyone else you find behind the house. I'll take care of the two at the front. Standard ops proto-cols: one tap and no noise." He turned to Logan. "You'll be our eyes and ears. Anything changes, inform us immediately." He looked at everyone in turn. "We'll be connected all the time. Once everyone outside is taken care of, Olivia will secure the building from the back and Elijah from the front. I'll go inside. One-eight-zero seconds, in and out. If the connection breaks or I'm not out in three minutes, Elijah will follow me inside. If you see anyone except Majeed, shoot to kill. Any questions?" They all shook their heads.

# CHAPTER 16

Outside, night had started to descend on a city still reeling with the grief and shock of the blast. No terrorist group had as yet come forward to take responsibility for the gruesome killings. The police were clueless, politicians were trying to rake in political gains from the tragedy, and the media was blaming everyone they could imagine. Wick was only concerned about how this circus would affect their ability to accomplish the mission.

The number of uniforms patrolling the city had increased. Logan took extra precautions and drove within the speed limit. Staying under the radar was important.

The team was ready for any eventuality but preferred not to engage proactively. Logan was using internal roads and alleyways to maneuver through the grief-stricken city. Luckily, they did not find any roadblocks.

.  .  .

Logan braked as they reached the marked location after an hour's drive.

Olivia, Elijah and Wick got out and started walking briskly towards the target location. Wick was carrying the same Glock-26 with an Octane K-45 suppressor that he had taken to the convention center.

The three shadows covered ground rapidly under the moonless sky. The scarcity of streetlights allowed them to run without arousing suspicion. As they moved closer to the target, Wick felt anger rising in his gut. He had reasons to be angry. But right before a critical mission, it could be fatal for him and his team. Yet he couldn't shake his feelings.  This intermittent surge of emotions was a new territory for him. His anger combined with nerves before a big mission was turning him into a wreck.

The three of them navigated the deserted streets in less than ten minutes and took cover behind a brick wall.

The house stood silent in the dark, moonless night. The lights were out, and a casual passerby would assume everyone inside was already asleep. But Wick and his team knew better.

Luckily for them, the security details around the house appeared light. Majeed didn't expect any attack on him tonight or any other night. He was not a terrorist in Iran, and he knew that the USA didn't have the courage to hunt him on his own soil.

.  .  .

"Logan, any changes in the positions? Over," Wick said on the microphone.

"None. Over," Logan responded.

"On three." Wick used the fingers of his right hand for the count-down, then started to sprint towards the house.

# CHAPTER 17

Wick arced around to reach the front of the house. Crouching in the bushes, he could see the two gunmen guarding the front entrance.

Olivia and Elijah remained in the same position behind the brick wall, waiting for Wick's confirmation about his position. Once he was settled, Olivia sprinted to her position, followed by Elijah.

"We're in position," Elijah confirmed his arrival.

"Target in range. Over," Wick said

Sitting alone in the shadow of the bushes, Wick found his body trembling with rage. He looked at his right hand, his gun hand. It shook as it rested on his thigh. He tried but couldn't get it to stop. He felt nauseated, sick enough to vomit.

.   .   .

*Go time was in four minutes.*

Sitting in a crouched position, staring down the block at the house where Majeed was, he closed his eyes to conjure images of the men inside but got nothing. All he got was the face of the boy who had blown himself up and the thought of the two US soldiers burned to death. He shook his head to clear it.

"Wick, you ready?" His earphone crackled. It was Olivia.

"Yes," Wick said without skipping a beat. He looked at his trembling hand, and then back at the door where the two gunmen were standing lethargically, waiting for nothing. They were probably thinking how long the night was going to be. They weren't expecting a hit tonight. Wick and his team had the crucial element of surprise.

The building was an old, rambling, two-story house, a sufficient distance from the city. The lights inside were out. Either everyone inside was asleep or they were doing things that needed the cover of darkness.

"Hit hard. Hit fast. Leave nothing to chance. Over," Wick said in his mouthpiece. His last bit of advice before the hit.

"Copy that. Over." Olivia and Elijah spoke in unison.

. . .

"I'll take the left tango. Over," Elijah whispered again.

"Rightmost tango and the middle one. Target in range,' Olivia stated her position.

Logan heard everything from the minivan, his heartbeat racing to triple digits. He was still relatively new to such missions. The adrenaline gave him jitters. He pressed hard against the earphones to not miss any whispers.

"When I say three. Over," Wick muttered.

"Ready," said two voices in unison.

"One... two... three."

Three bullets pierced the stillness with a muzzle velocity of a thousand feet per second. Three small, symmetrical holes appeared in three skulls. Three dead bodies. Before they hit the ground, there were two more shots. Two more heads. Two more thudding sounds. All this in less than a three seconds. The sound of the bodies hitting the ground was absorbed by the still-ness of the night. For the next few minutes, three pairs of eyes remained glued to the house for any sign of movement from any direction. No one came out to check.

. . .

Wick jumped to his feet and sprinted towards the door. Olivia and Elijah ran and took their positions as planned.

Nearing the house, he scanned the area for any potential surprise.

Nothing worth worrying about.

Reaching the door, he pushed it slightly. It was bolted from within. He circled to check for any other entry. He checked with Olivia and Elijah too. The front door was the only access point to the house. Shooting the lock open would compromise the surprise element of the attack. He had to knock. He updated Olivia and Elijah about the situation. They nodded, alert.

Wick's Ka-Bar blade was out. He didn't want to use a gun where a knife would do the trick. Also, an open door would do no good in case of a gunshot, however suppressed the sound might be. For speed and silence, the knife was his best bet.

Wick knocked on the door twice and stayed put. Footsteps approached from inside. Wick hoped there wasn't any code-word for opening the door. Someone like Majeed wasn't a typical target. He was a religious figurehead who was never linked directly to any terror attack in public. The thin security detail had made it clear that he was not even expecting an attack like this one, at least not today. The footsteps reached the door. Wick kept to the right side of the door. It was always better to be on the side in case the host was revealed to be a maniac with a gun.

The door opened and a familiar face appeared. Farhad squinted in the dark. Wick wasted no time in slicing the blade through his neckline, followed by two more cuts. Then with his left hand, he grabbed Farhad's shirt to prevent the deadweight from falling on the ground. He dragged the body outside and laid him to the left side of the door.

"I'm going in," he whispered into his mic. "Time your watches to one-eighty.'

# CHAPTER 18

Wick's eyes had already adjusted to the dark. His Glock was out, along with a pencil-sized flashlight in a surefire hold in his other hand, not yet lit. Moving ahead slowly, Wick rapidly considered his options.

Considering the obvious age of the house, its rusticity, and the lack of any apparent alarm keypads, he doubted that the house had a security system.

When he slowly pushed the door inward, one hinge rasped, and at once a voice arose from deeper within the house. Wick froze on the threshold, but then he realized that he was listening to an advertisement coming from a radio. An AK-47 lay on the table in the large, dimly lit living room. The room was deserted.

The wind whistled into the house, rattling a wobbly lampshade and threatening to betray him, so he closed the door. The radio voices came down from the first floor, to his left.

The living room had hunter-green leather armchairs with foot-stools, a tartan-plaid sofa on large ball feet, rustic oak-end tables, and a section of bookshelves that held perhaps three hundred volumes. The decor was thoroughly but not aggressively masculine.

Where he had been expecting pervasive clutter as evidence of Majeed's seriously disruptive mind, there was neatness. Instead of filth, cleanliness. Even in the shadows, Wick could see that the room was well dusted and swept. Rather than being burdened with the stench of death, the house was redolent of lemon-oil furniture polish and a subtle pine-scented air freshener.

Selling tax services and then various food items, the radio voices bounced enthusiastically down the stairs. Farhad had it cranked up too loud; the volume level seemed wrong to Wick, as if someone was trying to mask other sounds. There was another sound, and after a moment he recognized it: a shower. That was why the radio was set so loud. Someone was in the shower, listening to the music. Maybe Majeed.

Wick smiled at his luck. As long as Majeed was in the shower, Wick could search the house without the risk of being discovered.

.   .   .

Wick hurriedly crossed the front room to a half-open door, went through, and found a kitchen. Canary yellow ceramic tiles with knotty-pine cabinets. On the floor, gray vinyl tile speckled with yellow and green and red. Well-scrubbed. Everything in its place. Taped to the side of the refrigerator was a calendar already turned forward to April, with a black and white photograph of a man Wick couldn't recognize instantly. He tore the picture and stuffed it into his pocket, making a mental note of checking it once he was out of there.

The normality of the house puzzled him; the gleaming surfaces, the tidiness, the homey touches, the sense that a person was still there who might walk in daylight on any street and pass for human despite the atrocities that he had committed.

*Don't think about it. Keep moving.*

Upstairs, the music had started again, but it was more muted in the kitchen than the living room. The noise of the running shower, though, was more apparent in the kitchen than in the living room, because the pipes were channeled through the rear wall of the old house. The water being drawn upward to the bathroom made an urgent, hollow, rushing sound through copper. Furthermore, the pipe wasn't tied down and insulated as well as it ought to have been, and at some point, along its course it vibrated against a wall stud: rapid knocking behind plasterboard. If that noise stopped abruptly, he would know that his safe time in the house was limited. In the subsequent silence, he could count on no more than a minute or two of grace while Majeed toweled off. Thereafter he might show up anywhere.

.    .    .

There was a door in the living room, under stairs. Wick turned the knob as quietly as he could and stepped inside with caution. Beyond lay a combination laundry and storage room: a washer, an electric dryer, boxes and bottles of laundry supplies were stored in an orderly fashion on two open shelves, and the air smelled of detergent and bleach.

The rush of water and the knocking pipe were even louder here than they had been in the kitchen. To the left, past the washer and dryer, was another door—rough pine, painted lime green. He opened it and saw stairs leading down to a basement. Wick's heart began to beat faster.

"There's a cellar here. I'm going down," he whispered.

Olivia and Elijah acknowledged in whispers.

Wick descended the stairs deliberately. The steps ended at a mid-sized hall with three doors.

He scanned the three doors closely. A sliver of light showed from under the one farthest from him. He decided to check the other two first. He opened the nearest door. It was dark within and Wick used the pencil flashlight over his Glock to search the room. It was empty.

He did the same with the other. Again, nothing. That left only one room.

"Last room in the basement. I'm going in. Over," he whispered in the mic.

Wick turned the knob slowly, careful not to make any sound, and pushed the door open. It swung inward. A man was standing with his back towards Wick, his buttocks gyrating. The man was oblivious that someone had entered the room. Wick's gun was pointed at the back of his head.

Wick took this opportunity to quickly scan the rest of the room to see if anyone else was lurking in the darkness. Behind him, the door clicked shut on its own. The sound alerted Majeed who turned. As soon as his eyes met the barrel staring at him, his face lost color. But he wasn't alone. From behind Majeed a pair of fearful, misty eyes also stared at the gun.

# CHAPTER 19

As soon Wick entered the room, he had sensed that Majeed wasn't alone. He was naked and his actions meant he had company.

It wasn't unusual for Wick to find his targets in vulnerable positions. Most of the time, the strike was planned that way, but sometimes he bumped into situations he hadn't envisioned. This was one of them.

He walked diagonally to get a fuller view of the person behind Majeed. He stopped in his tracks when he saw who it was.

Wick had expected a girl, but this girl was just a child. Possibly aged between four and five. Standing naked, her eyes full of terror, behind Majeed. No one said anything. Wick stared at the child in disbelief.

· · ·

Majeed saw an opportunity in the intruder's shock and jumped towards the other side of the bed. Wick sensed the movement a second later, instinctively moved his shooting hand in that direction and opened fire. The girl screamed, ducking to the floor. The bullets missed their target by millimeters.

Majeed's body touched the floor and his fingers closed around the AK-47 lying on the table near where he had landed. Wick had little time to think. The girl had put him off balance. He saw the weapon in Majeed's hand and pressed the trigger. His Glock coughed twice. The 9mm bullet pierced the soft tissues of Majeed's right palm.

Majeed jerked his hand back and yelled in pain. Wick covered the ground between them in a single stride and grabbed the AK-47. His Glock never left sight of Majeed. The suppressor had kept the noise at a minimum.

Wick checked his watch. Twenty-three seconds to go.

# CHAPTER 20

"Who are you?" Majeed cried looking at Wick.

Wick said nothing, looking at him with disgust. Wick raised his left hand and Majeed's unhurt hand instinctively covered his locket that had the pen drive.

"If you are American, then you cannot kill me. I am with you guys."

In his anger, Wick couldn't say anything.

"Believe me, you do not want to kill me. Call your boss. Ask them. They will vouch for me," Majeed stuttered through sobs, clutching his right hand.

. . .

"Who is on the second floor?"

"Second floor?"

"In the shower?"

"Farhad, maybe. I don't know." Majeed was surprised at the question.

"He can't be." Wick was sure about that.

"Why?" Majeed asked.

"Elijah, check the first floor," Wick said into the mic. "Who's the girl?" Wick ignored Majeed's question.

"I don't know. Farhad brought her. I don't know, where is he?"

"I killed him."

"You… you killed Farhad?" Majeed's eye widened with shock. "I can give you the information. There is an attack planned in DC."

"When?"

.  .  .

"On the fifth day from now."


"Where in DC?"


"Multiple targets."


"Keep talking."


"A few months ago, I got an assignment to prepare for a chemical attack in the capital," Majeed started to blabber nonstop. Wick kept listening in rapt silence, one eye on the child who was cowering in fear near the bed.


"Assignment from whom?" he asked when Majeed stopped speaking.


"I don't know. I spoke with a man on my secure line."


"That's not enough."


"I told you everything that I know."

.  .  .

Majeed's face was flushed. Wick knew Majeed knew more than he was telling.

Wick looked at the girl who had stopped crying and was now looking at the two men.

"Where are your clothes?" Wick asked her.

She pointed at the table on which the assault rifle was placed. Wick grabbed them and threw them to her.

"Wear them. Go outside and wait for me."

With her little fingers she wrapped herself in the clothes. At her age, she was quite deft at the handling herself. She got up and left the room. The door closed behind her.

"Take her," Majeed said, desperately. "She is good. I know…"

It was the wrong thing to say. Something inside Wick snapped, and his trigger finger fired a round into the Majeed's skull before the latter could even finish his sentence. There was no blood, no guts, no graphic explosion of gore. Just a well-placed shot that crumpled his body, killing him instantly.

# CHAPTER 21

By killing the target, he was supposed to bring home alive, Wick had already ruined the mission, but personally he suddenly found the peace he had been seeking earlier.

He hurriedly scanned the space and checked the only wardrobe in the room. Majeed's naked body lay motionless on the floor. Wick took out his cell phone and captured the image of Majeed's dead body. He then filmed the room along with the dead body. Then grabbed the only thing that was on Majeed's naked body – the shiny locket. He stuffed anything useful he could find in the room into his pockets. There wasn't much. It was a bare room with just the bed and wardrobe.

He checked his watch; he was already a minute over the deadline. He came out of the room and found the girl waiting for him.

.   .   .

He heard footsteps. "Elijah, is that you? Over," he said, his gun pointing at the stairs.

"Affirmative. Over," Elijah's voice said over the earpiece.

Elijah appeared in the hallway. Wick lowered his gun as soon his eyes met Elijah's. Elijah followed suit. Looking at the girl, Elijah immediately realized that the mission had gone off-script, but he said nothing. This was not the time for questions. It was time to move.

"Rest of the building is clear." Elijah confirmed.

"We're leaving." Wick ordered.

"Where is Majeed?" Elijah asked.

"Dead," Wick responded. Along with Elijah, everyone else listening gasped at the information. Capture him alive—that had been their strict directive.

"Esm e shoma chist?" Wick asked the girl's name in Farsi, his calm voice belying the fact that he had just disobeyed direct orders by killing the man he had been ordered to bring home alive.

·  ·  ·

175

"Hiba," the girl responded.

"Where are you from? Shoma ahleh koja hastid?"

Hiba didn't answer this time.

"Where is your mother?" Wick changed the question, again speaking in Farsi.

She pointed above.

"Let's take you to your mother." Wick offered her his hand. She clutched his fingers tightly, and they walked towards the stairs.

"Logan, approach the house. Over," Wick whispered in his earpiece.

"On it. Over," Logan responded.

Once the three emerged from the door, they found Olivia waiting for them. She looked at Hiba but said nothing. The moonlit night was calm. Hiba looked confused. Her mother was nowhere in sight. She looked back at Wick with moist eyes. Wick didn't know what to do with the girl. No one did.

.   .   .

Logan stopped the minivan near the house. Hiba looked at Wick with curiosity.

"We need to find your mother. He will help us." Wick spoke in Farsi, pointing at Logan behind the wheel.

Hiba got inside. Wick followed and closed his door.

Elijah and Olivia got into the van next. Logan pressed the pedal and the van moved forward.

"Who is she?" Logan asked finally.

"Hiba," Elijah replied.

"Where is her family?" Logan asked.

"She doesn't know," Elijah replied.

Olivia stared at Wick who was unusually quiet, keenly checking the locket, the photos and the documents he had recovered from Majeed's room. The girl was sitting close to him, watching everyone in the van with curiosity. The team had a lot of questions about what had happened in the building, but this was not the time and place. The priority now was taking the girl to someone or someplace safe, if not her mother. Although this was not the mission they had planned, Wick had left them with no other option.

"We can leave her outside one of the nearby houses and let them call the police," Elijah suggested. Logan and Olivia nodded. Hiba looked at Wick who was staring out of the mini-van. She knew they were talking about her but unable to under-stand English.

"Wick, you concur?" Olivia asked.

Wick didn't respond. His mind was racing, thinking of ways he could help Hiba find her family and handle Majeed's death. He had not thought this through when he'd killed Majeed, but he knew he could not take the girl with him. She belonged here, and he belonged nowhere.

"Logan, stop the vehicle."

"What happened?"

"Elijah, you take the wheels. I need Logan to do something." Wick's voice had an urgency that brooked no dissent.

Logan stopped the minivan and got out. A couple of minutes later the minivan was again in motion with Elijah at the wheel.

.  .  .

"Get me the cell number of someone from the UNICEF Office in Tehran, someone who deals with homeless or lost kids. Also, I need an email for all the news channels and newspapers in Iran."

"What email?"

"Thinking on it. You got the number?"

"Almost," Logan said.

"Olivia, you find the office address of the Tehran-PressTV channel. We'll leave her there."

Olivia didn't know what was going on in Wick's mind, but she checked the GPS. The office was a thirty-minute drive from their current position.

"Now I need you to send two emails from two masked servers, spaced thirty-one minutes from each other. The first email on Hiba will go to Tehran PressTV. The second email on Majeed's death will go to all news channels." Taking the number from Logan, Wick said "Write this in the email: 'Majeed was shot dead by masked men a few minutes ago. I'll send a video soon.' Then attach this photo in the email. This will go second." He sent the photo of Majeed that he took after killing him. "Now, in the first email, write: 'A girl is waiting at the reception of your building. She is looking for her family. Please help her to unite with her family. The world is watching you. Allah is watching you.' Save these two emails. I'll tell you when to send the first one. The second one should be triggered after thirty-one minutes. And use Majeed's full name."

Logan, Olivia and Elijah looked surprised. What video proof was Wick talking about? Logan kept typing. Once sure of the email's language he showed it to Wick who made a few changes and then saved the draft. He would send it when the time was right.

Hiba was beginning to look sleepy. In the comfortable tempera-ture inside the van, she had temporarily forgotten that her mother was not with her. Yet all this while she had not left Wick's arm. Her tiny little fingers had an unusually tight grip that surprised Wick.

After traveling for more than thirty minutes, the four-wheeler stopped opposite the building where the Tehran-PressTV office was located. The street was deserted but the office lights were still on. The news never stops, be it any country. Wick quickly scribbled something on a piece of paper.

Olivia opened the door on her side and, before getting out of the van, covered her face and head. Wick did the same before getting out with Hiba. He knew these buildings could have CCTVs.

The cold night air had woken Hiba, and she looked at the building with childlike curiosity. Standing on the cold deserted street, she looked up at Wick. She was scared, but not as much as before. Looking at her, no one could say that she had just been rescued from such a traumatic experience.

Wick crossed the street with Hiba. Olivia remained in place.

The building's entrance was deserted too, but the well-lit reception area meant that people were still there.

"Wait here. Someone will come and take you to your mother," Wick told Hiba in Farsi. She nodded. There was no resistance from her. Perhaps she too sensed she could go no further with her savior. This was where they had to part ways. Olivia, too, was watching Hiba with surprise. Her composure and her understanding of the situation at this tender age was amazing. She had been worried that the girl would create a ruckus and it would be difficult to leave her anywhere without attracting unwanted attention, but it appeared she had been wrong.

Wick took out his burner cell and called the city's emergency social service hotline number–123. He reported that a girl child was stranded away from her family and was currently at the Tehran-PressTV office. That is where they had found the girl. The operator assured them that two people from his team would reach the spot within thirty minutes. Wick then dialed the number of the local police station and repeated the same story about Hiba. The officer on the phone initially showed reluctance to do anything at this time of the night, but as soon as Wick mentioned the address of Tehran-PressTV, the officer agreed to reach the venue within minutes. The police and the media had always been strange bedfellows. Their hatred towards each other was matched only by their need of each other. Wick didn't stop there; his next call was to the man in the UNICEF office in Tehran at the number Logan had given him. The man picked up the phone and promised immediate action. As soon as Wick disconnected the phone, Hiba asked, "What is your name?"

Wick hesitated. She kept her gaze at him. "Samuel," he said.

"Samuel!" she repeated and smiled. He smiled back.

Olivia came from behind and nudged him to move. Once people started coming, everything would start going downhill. Wick knew the risks.

"Go and stand there," he said to Hiba, pointing at the reception table. Hiba turned and looked at the place, then turned back. "Knock on that table like this." He showed her how to do it. "Someone will come and take you with them. They will show you on TV and your mother will come to get you. Don't be scared, I will be watching you. You'll be safe." Wick gave a genuine smile. Hiba smiled back, trusting the man who had rescued her. He put the paper he had scribbled on a few moments ago in her hand and closed her fist so she wouldn't lose it. He then nudged her, and she walked towards the reception, occasionally turning around to see if Wick was still there. Wick whispered in his mic, "Send the email on Hiba."

Logan complied.

.   .   .

Wick remained where he was, in a bid to reassure Hiba till she reached the reception.

At the reception, Hiba's first two knocks on the table yielded nothing, but then a woman's silhouette appeared.

Hiba extended her hand to give her the paper. The woman looked at the child with surprise and then read the note.

"My name is Hiba. My mother is missing. Police and UNICEF are on their way here to help me find her. They will be here in a few minutes. Can you stay with me till then?"

"How did you come here?" The woman gave her a motherly smile.

The girl turned and signaled at the road. The woman looked in the direction. There was no one there. Wick was gone. The van was gone.

She looked back at Hiba. "Are you hungry?" The girl nodded in affirmation. "Let's go and get you something to eat," the woman offered.

# CHAPTER 22

Inside the minivan, Wick sat in silence, waiting for the second email to be triggered. Logan looked at Olivia to say something.

The team was baffled by the way Wick was going about Majeed's case. As if he didn't care about orders. They couldn't say much to him; they didn't know him well enough. They had heard about him, of course, but this was the first time they were working with him and, watching him from close quarters, his mannerisms worried them. There would be an inquiry on this, and that would include them, too. They were his accomplices in the mission. What would they say? They had little or no information of what had transpired between Majeed and Wick alone in that room in those crucial moments when Wick had decided to shoot him. Hiba was gone and, anyway, they didn't know enough Farsi to have even asked her basic questions. So that opportunity was long gone.

"Wick, what did Majeed tell you before dying?"

.   .   .

Wick told them about the attack briefly.

"Wick, you sure you want to send this email. I think you should talk to Helms first." Olivia sounded both worried and skeptical.

"I'll talk to him when the time comes. I know what you guys are thinking, but I'm alone in this, no one will point a finger at you. There will be an inquiry and I want each one of you to say whatever you think is right. I'm ready for the consequences but I don't want to burden you guys with my conscience."

"But why send an email and raise this shitstorm?" Logan asked.

Wick looked at him for a moment and took the image out of his pocket.

"Do you know who this man is?" Wick extended the image he had grabbed from the refrigerator. They studied it in the dim light of the van.

"No."

"Baitullah Maksud."

.   .   .

"Baitullah Maksud!" The two words captured everyone's attention. They looked at the picture with renewed interest.

"This is the only image of Maksud that US intelligence agencies ever managed to get their hands on."

"Where did you find this?"

"In Majeed's house."

"You think there's a connection between Majeed and Maksud?"

"I've a theory."

"Care to elaborate?" Olivia said curtly.

"Few years ago, a group of German doctors visited Iraq on a humanitarian mission. Their group was attacked. While a few of them managed to escape unhurt, a few doctors from that group were abducted. The German government managed to get them released safely, except one: a German surgeon who died of a heart attack in mysterious circumstances."

"I remember that," Elijah said without looking back.

·  ·  ·

"Maksud's terrorist group was identified as the one behind the attacks and the abduction. This image of Maksud was taken a week before that attack. And after this attack, he went underground. His terrorist group is still active though."

"What does this have to do with Majeed?"

"Before embarking on this journey tonight, I asked my contacts in the NSA and CIA for intel on the group who abducted and burned the two American soldiers."

"And?"

"Ninety-three percent chances are that Maksud's group did it."

Everyone in the van knew what ninety-three percent meant in their profession. Some of them had executed missions even with far lower chances of certainty. Ninety-three meant that the intel was extremely credible.

"You think Majeed had some connection with the killing of the US soldiers?" Elijah asked. He was now interested in where this was going.

"I asked my contacts to check the coordinates of Farhad from the day the US soldiers were abducted. He had always been at locations close to where, per our estimates, the US soldiers were possibly kept, till the day we lost track of them. That was a week ago."

"Why wasn't this done earlier? How can the agencies miss a man like Farhad?" Elijah asked.

"Because our complete focus was on Majeed. He's the face for us. Everyone, including me, thought that Farhad was just a side-kick, but when I saw that Farhad wasn't with Majeed at the convention, I thought of checking his digital footprints."

"So, you think Majeed and Farhad are both working for Maksud?"

"I think Farhad is working for Maksud."

"What do you mean?"

"I think Majeed is Baitullah Maksud, and the German doctor who supposedly died of a heart attack was in fact murdered."

"How are these two things connected?"

"First, the German doctor who died was a world-renowned plastic surgeon. Second, Majeed came into prominence only after Maksud was gone. If you check Majeed's history, there is a backstory about him, but there are no photos before a certain time which can corroborate that backstory. Due to international pressure, Maksud probably decided to take on a new identity, and the one who could help him do it at the time was the German surgeon. My assumption is that the attack on the German doctors was also planned to hide the fact that there was a plastic surgeon in the group, so that no one would see this connection. And the plan worked because no one did point it out."

"This seems very farfetched," Olivia said. She wasn't convinced.

"I told you this is just a theory. I'm still awaiting a few more details to connect the dots," Wick responded without taking any offence.

"Why didn't you tell us? We could be of help to you," Logan said, ignoring Olivia's skepticism.

"If I had told you, and if my theory bombs, then your careers would be compromised. You were assigned only for this mission. Maksud is a different ball game altogether, and I'll deal with it my way."

"Then why tell us now?" Olivia asked.

"I think I owe you guys at least this much, if nothing more.

Mentally I'm ready for anything from here on but cannot expect the same from you."

Logan checked his email server. The second email about Majeed's killing had been triggered a minute ago. He looked at Wick who checked his watch and tacitly understood what Logan's expression meant.

To put things in motion, Wick made a few calls from his burner cell. The reaction to the revelation that Majeed was dead meant that the things would move very fast. News in Iran already had a field day in progress. First the blast and then Majeed's death, two big breaking news items within a few hours of each other was something that would need no further push.

The minivan raced towards the safehouse. From there, they would leave for Turkmenistan separately. And then to Maryland, USA. What they didn't know was that Wick had just changed his plans. He had decided to stay in Iran for a few more weeks.

He knew now that the news of Majeed's death was out, Maksud's terror group would start squirming, if indeed Majeed had been their leader. Wick had enough ears on the ground to map this activity, but for that he needed to be here in person. But before anything else, he needed to convince Helms, and he wanted to do that without the distraction of Olivia, Logan and Elijah's questioning eyes. They didn't need to know he would be staying.

. . .

Wick checked the live news telecast on the Tehran-PressTV. Hiba was already on live TV and anchor was talking about her missing family. At least the process of finding Hiba's family had been set in motion before this tiny news drowned in the avalanche of Majeed's news.

Logan checked other news channels; they had all started to broadcast the image of Majeed that he had emailed them from the encrypted server. Even if anyone found the server, its location was Tehran. He had made sure that nothing from the email would point to the US. Not only that, the email about Hiba and the email on Majeed couldn't be linked to each other. That would have made life difficult for that little girl.

After checking the news on multiple channels, Wick dictated the next email with the video that was promised in the first email. Once Majeed's news was live on TV, he sent the next one too. After everything was done, Logan closed his laptop.

* * *

Elijah stopped the minivan in a deserted alley two-and-a-half miles from the safe house.

Everyone dumped their weapons and everything that could get them in trouble into an open tin box and torched them along with the minivan. Then they took out their American passports and IDs. Fakes, but the airlines wouldn't know that. Once they were sure that everything was in order, they separated from each other. Oliva and Logan left first. Wick and Elijah waited a few minutes before Elijah took off. Wick waited for Elijah to disappear before heading towards a secluded corner. He had to talk to Helms now.

Wick made contact with William Helms, his boss, on the first attempt.

"There is a chemical attack planned in DC in four days." Wick repeated whatever Majeed had told him. He had already given the pen drive to Logan who had uploaded the data to the NSA server for decryption. Helms listened to everything in silence without interruption.

"Where is Majeed?" he asked finally, after Wick had finished.

"Dead," Wick responded.

"How?" There was a slight hint of a surprise in his voice, but not an overt reaction.

"I shot him," Wick spoke in a plain tone. No apology, no guilt, no nothing.

"We needed him alive." Helms said in a matter-of-fact tone.

Wick said nothing.

.   .   .

"What now?" Helms continued. He had considered the possibility that Majeed might get killed in the operation, but Wick's response meant that he had had the opportunity to capture him alive and had still chosen not to.

"The support team is following the itinerary. I need more time here."

"Why?"

Wick explained his plan and theory to him.

"How confident are you of this theory?"

"About seventy percent."

"That's not enough," Helms said.

"That is why I have to stay here to get the evidence."

"You've made up your mind?" Helms asked.

"Yes."

.   .   .

"What if it doesn't pan out the way you think it will?"

"I'm ready to face any inquiry or termination."

"I'll still need a full report in my email inbox. Don't mention anything about your theory right now."

"You'll get it."

"Be safe."

"I will." Wick disconnected the call.

The attack on US soil was troubling, but Wick was confident that it would now be taken care of.

# CHAPTER 23

William Helms was pacing back and forth in his office. He had called an emergency meeting, and also informed the CIA, Homeland Security, and the FBI about the potential attack. They had already started to raid the locations specified in the data Wick's team had uploaded. Till now Wick's intel was on the mark.

But there was something else. He had allowed Wick far too much latitude, and this angered him. Although he hadn't shown any of it during the call, and while much of his anger was directed at Wick, a lot of it was also directed at himself. How had he not seen the signs earlier?

This place, this operation, all of it was his responsibility. People had tried to warn him as respectfully or as forcefully as they could, but his days were filled with hundreds of other pressing issues of national importance. And he had developed a blind spot when it came to Wick's abilities and his mental strength.

Especially on the operational side of things. He'd known Wick longer than anyone else at TF-77. He knew his long list of talents as well as his short but potent list of faults. There'd been a few bumps over the years, but there was never an occasion when Wick had let him down. He still remembered the day Wick was recruited. He had been in his early twenties, fresh out of tours from Afghanistan and Iraq, trained and thirsty to reach greater heights, ready for a fight. Helms had seen his hunger firsthand when they had operated together on a mission involving the extraction of a North Korean General. Wick had a real aptitude for mayhem. He was talented, remarkably perceptive, favored with an elephant memory and calculative; a lot of other things too, some good and some bad. But one thing was undeniable— he knew how to get to his targets, engage them, upset them, get them, and somehow make it back with nothing more than a few scratches. Wick was meant for this deadly business. He was an artist. Minimum bloodshed and maximum impact. He rarely used bullets, and always focused on figuring the best possible way to isolate the target before pouncing. He had few friends in the TF-77 group, but instead of choosing a desk job and falling into a safe rut, he had chosen his current life.

Wick had never thought much about his own life. He was always ready to jump into the eye of the storm. When he landed in a new place, he headed straight for the rough part of town. He got to know the prostitutes, the barkeeps and, most importantly, the black marketeers who despised their overlords. He was the best field operative they had. Indispensable.

Tonight, however, the director was having his doubts. Looking back, he could see where the mistakes had been made. He had allowed Wick to create a personality cult down here. Even on this mission, he had been adamant about going solo until Helms had intervened. It was time to correct the mistakes.

"Elena, what do you propose?" The director looked at TF-77's deputy director, who was sitting in his office examining a thick file about Wick's failure to get Majeed alive. "What does the protocol say?"

"We should wait for him to come back with credible intel," she replied.

"But the rules say that there has to be an inquiry on this."

"Yes."

"Who do you suggest should head the inquiry committee?"

"David Scott would be a good choice," Elena said.

Helms knew about David. The man's reputation preceded him— tough as nails and unwavering in his commitment to TF-77. He shrugged, indicating he was fine with the decision.

"Elena, start the work but go slow. I want to give Wick a chance to redeem himself. If his theory is correct, we don't want to look stupid. Give him enough time before you conclude anything. Supervise this yourself. I don't want to be involved since this is about Wick, but I would like to see the final report before it goes into the records."

"Okay," Elena said.

"What about the White House? They must have checked the news on Majeed's death."

"The Secretary of Defense is not happy, but his priority is stopping this chemical attack. This botched mission has already put our position with Iran in jeopardy. Russia has joined Iran in insinuating that the killing was our doing. The President has denied any links and has also promised his support to bring the perpetrators to book even though the two countries are not on good terms. Looks like this will take a long time to go down, and not without some collateral damage. We have also found some incriminating evidence of the attack originating from Iran and we'll respond at the right time. At the moment though, the White House is still working on a foolproof strategy to corner Iran."

"Elena, everything eventually comes down to two things: influence and money. One of those will be used to settle this as well."

Elena said nothing. The director looked out the window. Why had Wick allowed this to happen?

# CHAPTER 24

Wick walked down an empty corridor. The plain white walls were designed to give the building an air of truthfulness, even as they hid the dirty secrets of surveillance and espionage. His appointment with the director was in fifteen minutes. He had just got out of his hearing with the inquiry commission. David Scott had been prepared to the hilt and had taken a lot of time grilling Wick, but Wick's poker face had given him nothing more than the routine answers he was expecting.

Right after the hearing, Wick was told Helms wanted to see him.

* * *

Helms squinted through the windscreen of the Suburban as the SUV turned into the empty fast lane, accelerating past a Kia. The skyline was clear and cloudless, but his mind was swirling with questions. He put on his shades to avoid the glare. Sitting in the passenger seat, he opened his laptop to check the news. It was filled with Iran's accusations against America. The US had taken the counteroffensive by showing incriminating evidence against Iran in the chemical attack which Iran called a conspiracy. A battle was ongoing between the US and Iran through media headlines.

The White House was doing its best, of course. A statement had already been made denying any connection with the cleric or the blast. The President had also strongly condemned the massacre and given his assurance that everything would be done to help Iran in its investigation, but in return he wanted Iran to hand over the culprits who planned the attack on the USA. Iran had vehemently denied any such terror group operating from its soil, but America remained insistent, and it decided to remain so till the news of the cleric would die down.

Helms asked the driver to turn on the radio. After the weather forecast of searing heat, the lead item in the news was the murder of the cleric. The motive for the killing had not been found. It was "senseless and shameless," an Iranian policeman concluded.

Helms knew this wasn't true. It wasn't senseless, and it wasn't a mistake. The operation had been in the works for a long time, one hundred and seventeen days to be exact—identifying security details, cultivating targets, understanding their routine, gaining the trust of their aides in Iran, followed by weeks setting up the set pieces.

·  ·  ·

The objective had almost been successfully achieved, but then it wasn't. The director had seen botched operations, but this was an operation that had been botched deliberately.

This raised doubts over the performance of the man who had carried out the operation. The fact that it was Sam Wick was troubling. It had been the director's operation—a direct chain of command from the top. He knew the targets; he was involved in the planning. He had stopped doing that for almost all the other missions, but he had done it for this one. A decision had been made, within the walls of the Oval Office, that Majeed knew too much and he needed to be brought in. That decision was stamped with the presidential seal and passed on to NSA to be closed. It was critical, and that's why Sam had been selected to close the file.

As the Suburban entered the headquarters, the director reviewed his preparation. He thought hard about whether there had been any flaw in the original plan. No, the plan was faultless. The problems were all of Wick's making. The dead man would give Iran's secret service agencies a strong personal motive to locate the killer; religion and terrorism were strong motives to accomplish things in any country, and here the slain man combined both. It would make them more tenacious and less likely to shelve the investigation when the trail went cold, as Helms knew it would.

The SUV slowed and turned into the parking lot at the National Security Agency headquarters, Fort Meade, Maryland.

.   .   .

TF-77 wasn't run from this building, but Helms' office was located there, and that's why the inquiry was taking place there.

Mirrored and forbidding, the NSA campus stood like a fortress surrounded by a moat of parking. The general public knew almost nothing about what happened inside. It was like a reminder that the environment of state security has taken dark turns over the last three decades. The architecture of the building was as compelling as it was unsettling—much like the J. Edgar Hoover, the FBI headquarters. Hundreds of cars were parked around the building, standing in for the thousands of intelligence workers inside—the serfs of the deep state, as it were. Fort Meade looked like it might be the end of the earth, an exurb you never hope to have reason to visit. Like the FBI Building, the NSA headquarters was a metaphor for the agency it hosted. Helms took the elevator to the fourth floor. The doors hissed opened, and he stepped out into the bustling open space beyond, full of analysts staring at large monitors and tapping keyboards, printers chattering and telephones ringing incessantly. He walked through the chaotic space to a corridor with gray tiles, white walls and red oak doors. The clamor behind him slowly faded to a gentle hum of activity. He pushed one of the doors open. Vanessa Lisbon, his private secretary, looked up from her computer. "Good morning, Director," she said.

"Morning, Captain," he said. "And what does this morning look like?"

"You're speaking to the Secretary of State at midday for an update on the Iran situation, and Sam Wick is waiting for you in your cabin, sir."

203

. . .

William Helms said nothing and kept walking. His office was a large room dominated by his desk at the center with minimal accessories to adorn it. A set of sofas clubbed around the table. There were no filing cabinets or anything that looked official. Sam stood at the wide window at the other end of the room looking outside. Helms paused for a moment and regarded him. Dressed in plain white shirt and black trousers he looked lean.

"Good morning, Sam," Helms said.

"Morning, sir."

"Take a seat."

He watched as Wick sat down. His eyes were impenetrable. He looked a little weary, maybe from the nonstop grilling and lack of sleep, but overall, he was still sharp. As always, Wick was dressed sharply, perfectly groomed. Over time, Helms had decided that these things do matter, but only in diplomatic situations, which this was not.

"Anything you would like to say about the mission?"

"Everything is in my final report." Wick was talking about the final report he had submitted a week ago, corroborating his theory and the evidence.

. . .

"Nothing to add?"

"Nothing."

"The only good news amid all this is that the girl... what was her name?

"Hiba."

"She is now with her family."

"I know."

"It took time, but they found her family."

"Yes." This time director felt that there was a slight hint of a smile on Wick's lips, but he couldn't be sure.

"Have you had any contact with Olivia, Logan or Elijah after the mission?"

"No."

. . .

"Any idea what they could have said during their testimonies?"

"No." Wick's responses gave Helms no room to maneuver further.

"The inquiry will take another week to conclude."

"You did good with Maksud. Once the team analyzes the evidences in your report, we can use it to strengthen our case against Iran."

Wick said nothing but the director could tell that he didn't care much about it. He had done his job and now cared nothing about it.

"I'm sorry but the inquiry will still go on for not following orders."

"I understand."

"Your future in the agency depends on it."

"I understand," Wick said, looking blankly at Helms.

# CHAPTER 25

Ten days later

Wick sat at the window of his apartment, overlooking the street. He had been asked to stay home while the inquiry was in progress. He had not raised a question on why he was being grounded. He knew the protocols. They had called him for a hearing, and after that he had to stay put.

He had no friends, no family, no one to call and talk to about his feelings. Even if there had been someone, he doubted he would have reached out.  What could he tell them? His was not a regular job, and he wasn't a regular guy. It was better this way. Fight for yourself and live for yourself—it was easier to focus. And focus meant a better survival ratio.

He knew that his house was bugged and everything he said would be heard by some analyst sitting in the black tomb, better known as the TF-77 headquarters. Every one of the agency's assets' houses and cars was bugged, and he knew that the agency continued this practice even after you left it. Only the agency didn't know that Wick knew.

Wick had said nothing for days. He didn't have a television. He didn't use the Internet and so had not opened his laptop since he came home. He didn't care about the news or anything else. He checked his cell occasionally but did not send anyone any messages or speak to anyone. It was as if he had gone mute. So much so, that the TF-77 team had had to send agents dressed like delivery boys or lost paper boys to ring his doorbell to see if he actually was in the apartment or not. It took him no time to see through their act, but he said nothing, just played along, politely helping them with their fake questions as best as he could.

Ignorance was bliss as far as the agency was concerned. The agency had to feel safe. And Wick made sure of that by making them believe that the collective heads in the agency were smarter than him. He didn't know what would happen if they knew he was usually miles ahead of them in the game, even when not on active duty. The reason was that he didn't want them to try new tactics which he would then have to waste time deciphering. That was trivial shit he cared nothing about. He just cared about sitting still as a sculpture for as long as he could. It was his way to test his limits. And knowing his limits made him win battles and rise to the occasion when he needed to.

He had had a meeting with Helms after his hearing and it had been uneventful, at least from his side. He was not perturbed by the radio silence that followed.

He knew that if he was to be terminated from the agency, there would be a target painted on his back, with all the agency's assets aiming to eliminate him ASAP. If he was reinstated, then his next mission would be one that he would have to fight hard to come out of alive. Either way, he would have to wrestle to survive, and he was ready for both.

It was all part and parcel of this job.

He was lost in his thoughts when his cell phone vibrated.

This was the first sound he had heard coming from his cell in several days. He gently picked up the phone. *1 new email.*

He plugged in his access code and opened the application.

There was a one-liner email waiting for him. *Acknowledge mission specifics.*

There was a file attached. He opened the file and gave it a cursory read. Once satisfied that he had everything he needed to know, he typed two words—On it—and pressed the send button.

. . .

Two minutes later he received another email. In thirty minutes, his transport would be waiting for him in the back alley of his apartment building.

He didn't care what was in the final inquiry report, or how he had gotten out of it unscathed. All he cared about was that his next mission had just begun.

*The End*

* * *

# SINGULAR FORCE

## THE IMPOSSIBLE SHOT (A TF-77 SHORT)

## ABOUT SINGULAR FORCE

*Homing on his target, Eddie realized two things.*

*First, he only had one shot.*

*Second, it was an impossible shot.*

★ ★ ★

*What Readers are saying about TF-77 universe;*

★★★★★ *"One heck of an entertaining and intense ride... Fast, entertaining, suspenseful and action-packed... you will find yourself flying through and it will be hard to let it go!" - Amazon Review*

★★★★★ *"Fast paced read with a Kick-Ass hero you can't help rooting for." - Amazon Review*

★ ★ ★ ★ ★ *"Full of awesome action. I can't wait to read the next book" - Amazon Review*

★ ★ ★ ★ ★ *"Fast paced, lots of thrills. Highly entertaining." - Amazon Review*

\* \* \*

# SINGULAR FORCE

WAR TORN IRAQ

**Now**

Zeroing in on his target through the glass, Eddie realized two things.

First, he only had one shot.

Second, it was an impossible shot.

* * *

**60 minutes ago**

The rocky wall was soothingly cool and felt a tad bit reassuring behind his aching back. He rubbed his back gingerly against it to relieve the pain. But his eyes remained trained on the target village spread thinly below the vantage point. There was not a cloud in sight in the bright sky, nothing but the few eagles gliding over the desolate land.

Eddie Vicar was an El Paso stock, with black hair and vital, green eyes. He wasn't muscular like the other officers in his unit. His short height and wiry physique marked him out for ridicule from his colleagues and commanding officer.

He had been deployed in the long-drawn Iraq war that began in 2003 with the invasion of the country by a U.S.-led coalition that overthrew the government of Saddam Hussein. The war had ravaged the country and its cities, towns, and villages to their bare bones. 600,000 Iraqis had been killed in the conflict and that was just the figure for the first four years. No official data had been released after that. Maybe they had stopped counting because of the unprecedented numbers, or to avoid attracting flak from the human rights warriors.

Eddie shouldn't have been here. U.S. troops had been officially withdrawn from Iraq in 2009. But following the spread of radicalism in Iraq, the Syrian civil war and the territorial gains of ISIL, the U.S. government had re-deployed most of the withdrawn troops back in Iraq by 2014. Eddie was among those who got re-deployed. It wasn't that he didn't want to serve his country in whatever way he could. That had always been his long-cherished dream. What he hadn't considered, though, were the dire consequences of being perceived as "different" by a bunch of boys barely out of puberty, sent to a place like Iraq, far away from the safe surroundings of their homeland, and allowed to shoot and kill people with minimal supervision. It was that dark side of army life in a war-torn country like Iraq that no one spoke about and certainly no one had warned Eddie about.

The trigger-happy finger gave a different kind of high and very few people were able to control that power. When the fodder for their perversion started to thin in the field, they turned their sights to those among their own who were perceived as weak. That's when Eddie found himself at the receiving end of this dark side. And by the time he realized the depth of it, he was neck-deep in it. The situation deteriorated rapidly for him, thanks especially to one of the other snipers—Russell Wilson, who was the lead point man for taking out U.S. enemies in Iraq. Wilson was a big hunk from the redneck wilds of north-central Florida who had grown up hunting boar with his dad. His passion for hunting had made him a good sniper, but his daddy issues had turned him a bastard.

* * *

**24 hours ago**

Eddie balanced his falling body, face inches away from the dirt, in a push-up position.

It was 2 a.m. and the temperature was under thirty degrees. Summer days in Iraq were at the mercy of a relentless sun, but nights were generally freezing. Fortunately, air humidity was low.

Even in that cold, sweat poured from his face like rain, turning dirt into mud. He inhaled dust and muck every time he sucked in air. His muscles burned. Every inch of his body trembled with the effort. His rage wanted him to get up and square off with Wilson who'd spent the last eight weeks trying to bully him, break him. But his mind knew that would result in more such beatings from the rest of Wilson's platoon watching the bout. And frankly, he'd grown tired of those.

Soldiers in military fatigues, some without shirts, some in cargo shorts and polos, a few in nothing but boxers stood in a circle around the fighting pit.

The spectators, his commanding officer Morgan Heath among them, hurled obscenities at him. "You sonovabitch, get up and fight!"

Wilson's boot slammed into Eddie's ribs. "You don't belong to this team."

Eddie cried out in pain and hit the ground hard.

Wilson raised his knee and brought his boot down on the middle of Eddie's back like a victor posing for a photo.

Eddie struggled to breathe. His nostrils and lungs felt like they were full of dirt. Wilson was massive and heavy.

"Leave him," Heath said, finally.

Wilson shot Eddie a look of disgust but obeyed the direct order. Eddie remained on the ground, trying to control his breathing.

Wilson spat on the ground near his face. "Fuck you queer," he said and turned to leave. The rest followed him. The last one to leave was Heath.

Eddie lay there for a while and when everyone was gone, he slowly got up and sat on the ground staring at the spot still wet from Wilson's spittle.

* * *

**Now**

How do you take an impossible shot?

By getting the math right.

* * *

**55 minutes ago**

Perched on a high vantage point above the village and the compound, Eddie looked lost. The almost permanent grin on his boyish face was missing. A cursory glance at his face would have told any casual observer that Eddie had barely any feelings about this war, about his being there, about his environment. He was just there because he was ordered to be there.

But a closer look would reveal much more. His eyes had a lot to say. His shoulders were slouched. A faint bluish tinge covered most of the left side of his face. His left eye had a red clot. His rifle rested beside him. He cleaned it every day, though he had not yet had to use it in the six months since he had landed in Iraq.

But Eddie wasn't thinking about any of that. He was thinking about the village he was tasked to watch. Almost all the houses in the village were now deserted. The houses, where somebody —whole families—must have lived at some point in time.

What had happened to those people?

What had happened to those families?

Eddie brushed his thoughts aside. This was not the time and the place to think about such things. He still had some way to go in life before he had the luxury of pondering over such questions.

A gunshot not far away startled him from his reverie. His right hand instinctively went to his rifle. The gun's grip felt cool and reassuring in his hand, though he was careful to minimize his body movements. He was in a lot of pain, both physical and mental. But he couldn't let the pain show. His body wanted to, but his mind wouldn't allow it. He wasn't alone on the rocky roof. There were three other men, including Wilson and his CO, Morgan Heath.

* * *

**Now**

Eddie stretched his body carefully on the rocky surface. The pain intensified as he moved and the burning surface made it almost impossible for him to get into position, but he had to do it.

Below the village was deathly still. The wind was strong, blowing from left to right as Eddie crept up to a vantage point about thirteen hundred yards from the target.

Martinez Rovan, his sniping partner, lay beside him.

Rovan was small, slim, razor-sharp, without a wasted ounce of meat on his body. When he worked out in shorts and no shirt, he looked like a drawing of the human anatomy, each muscle group carefully delineated. Rovan had already zoned in on the target, hidden behind a fortified wall in a secure position some 1300 yards away, ready to shoot at anyone wearing a U.S. uniform.

There was no way Eddie could snare the enemy with the single shot that he had.

Eddie knew this as a fact. And he knew that his enemy knew this too.

* * *

**5 Hours ago**

"Gentlemen, this is a suicide mission." The resounding voice of Lieutenant Colonel Morgan Heath boomed in the hanger. "And that's why they chose us. We are the best in the business and now is the time to prove it."

Sitting at the back of the room, Eddie cringed inwardly at Heath's clumsy attempt at motivating his men.

Twenty others like Eddie were in the hangar. The team was a mix of Delta, Marines and the U.S. army. Eddie moved little throughout the briefing. He was in intense pain, but he was one of the three snipers at the base, so he had to be here. The lead sniper was Russell Wilson. The person Eddie hated the most apart from Morgan Heath.

Eddie tried to focus on gathering key insights from the briefing. The most important was that the mission was difficult—but not necessarily suicidal.

Morgan Heath was as hands-on and gung-ho a commander as there could be. He was not yet forty years old, and it was clear that the army was not the end of the line for him. Heath had rocketed up to his current rank, and his ambitions seemed to point toward a higher profile. He was handsome, fit, and over-the-top eager. That wasn't unusual for an army officer. But he also talked too much. And that wasn't Army at all.

Eddie looked at the TV screen behind Heath. A young man in a white bandana and stubbled face appeared on the screen. His eyes were striking—one brown and one green.

"This is our target," Heath said. "We don't know his real name, but in the video released by ISIS, he is called Torpedo. Our intel says that he represented Syria in the rifle shooting at the Summer Olympics. He is believed to have been born sometime around 1980 among a tribe of nomads in eastern Afghanistan or the tribal regions of western Pakistan; his family probably criss-crossed the border like it wasn't even there. ISIS runs in his veins. During the last few months, ISIS has released multiple videos of anti-US attacks and he features in several of them."

Heath flicked a button and a video appeared on the screen. It soon became clear why this video was being played. The clip started with Torpedo saying, "I have a gift for the U.S. President. I am going to kill American soldiers encroaching on our land, and millions around the world will watch. God is greater! God is greater!"

The sketchy video showed him making his way from a vehicle, and a series of separate scenes followed showing several individuals being shot with a rifle that seemed to be a Dragunov. Torpedo could shoot targets at a distance of anywhere between a few hundred to thousand-odd yards with extreme precision. Videos included parts of the actual clips taken during anti-US sniper operations with digital cameras mounted over the sniper rifle. Some of the shots executed by Torpedo were clearly beyond the capabilities of an ordinary shooter.

"It is still not proven completely whether Torpedo is a name given to this man in the video, or is it now a role shared among multiple individuals. It could also be a propaganda/media creation with a solid back story. The man became known after ISIS posted these online videos showing him shooting American soldiers. We have got intel that he is now in our region, and for the success of our upcoming missions he is a thorn that we need to take out." Heath paused for effect. He eyed everyone in the room. "This guy is bad news. Getting him will be the next best thing to taking down Osama bin Laden. Do you guys want to be heroes? Well, this is your chance."

Heath clicked a button on the remote. The photo on the screen changed. A split image appeared on the screen—on one side of the vertical border was an aerial shot of a compound just outside a small village; on the other side was a 3-D rendering of a house. The house was three stories tall, made of stone, and built against a steep hill.

Heath launched into a description of how the mission would go. "We will hit two targets today, and based on the intel we believe that our search for one will lead to another. This compound is target #1. The man who protects this compound, Torpedo, is our target #2. Our A and B teams will go in two choppers, eight in one and nine in the second. The choppers will set down in a field just outside the village, unload teams A and B, and then provide aerial support. Team C will include Wilson, Rovan, Eddie and me, and we will try to take out Torpedo from here." He pointed at a hill on the map.

"The village road that leads to this compound is narrow and we believe that Torpedo will be stationed there to stop us. We will take him out and then raid the compound. Once we get past Torpedo, A-Team will breach the walls, enter the compound, and assassinate any hostile inside. B-Team will hold the walls and the approach to the compound from the village. The choppers will then touch down again and extract all three teams. If for any reason the choppers cannot land again, the three teams will make their way to an old abandoned American forward firebase on a rocky hillside less than half a mile outside the village. Extraction will take place there, or the teams will hold the former base until extraction can occur."

\#

**35 minutes ago**

Eddie was still sitting behind Wilson, Heath, and Rovan, the other three members of Team C. Wilson was leading the team which wasn't surprising; he was Heath's go-to sniper.

Heath's presence was explained by the fact that killing Torpedo would be the highlight of the mission, not raiding an almost empty compound, and Heath had an excellent instinct for being in the right place at the right time in high-profile missions like this.

Wilson's spotter was Rovan, lying beside him, trying to zero in on the target. Once he had a lock on the target, it was Wilson's job to take Torpedo out.

Eddie was in the team as a backup sniper. He knew what he was and how he wouldn't be getting a shot. This was going to be a Wilson show.

Still, he took mental stock of his weapons. His weapons included an M24 Sniper Weapon System and an MP5 for close-quarter fighting. The guns were loaded, and he had extra magazines stuffed in his pockets. Besides, he had a SIG P226 sidearm, four grenades, a cutting, and a breaching tool.

His eyes scanned the unforgiving terrain before him, set against the backdrop of windswept mountains. The place seemed frozen in time like it had not progressed beyond the Stone Age. People occupying these terrains truly existed in a forgotten corner of the earth. The only technology this entire valley had was probably the automatic weapons and rockets snatched from the enemy.

The team was ready. The A and B squads had been dropped off at the designated locations. Now all that remained was to get Torpedo in the crosshairs, which was Rovan's job.

* * *

**25 minutes ago**

Teams A and B were now in position. No one was shooting at anyone yet. Heath's radio crackled to life. Team A's squad leader transmitted, "Ready to enter the village out-buildings."

Heath looked at Wilson, the man on whose shoulder this mission depended.

Wilson and his sniping partner Rovan were still looking for any sign of Torpedo.

"I need more time," Rovan hissed to Wilson.

Wilson nodded, his eyes fixed to the scope. "Tell 'em we got nothing yet. They have to wait," he told Heath.

Heath checked his comms as if pondering whether he should relay the message or not. Wilson was in charge of this situation. His shot would decide the next course of action. Sensing Heath's reluctance, Wilson looked up from his rifle optic.

Heath met his eyes for a long moment, but he was the first to blink. He reluctantly keyed his radio to transmit. "Team C copies, still waiting for movement. Stand by."

The teams below vanished back into hiding behind a cluster of trees. Rovan scanned the terrain again, half-expecting to see Torpedo getting ready to ambush any approaching American soldiers.

The village was still dead

And then in his crosshairs, he noticed a slight movement. A head popped out. It was a man behind a fortified, elevated position around 1300 yards away from where Team C was positioned. With just his head and shoulder visible and a howling wind blowing across, Torpedo knew the conditions were challenging for a long-range shooter. Challenging was an understatement. He was safe from any counterattack.

Rowan alerted Wilson, who checked too, then looked back at Heath.

"We've spotted him," Wilson said. "It's an impossible shot from here. We need to get closer. Need to gain more ground."

Heath discussed the situation with the Squad leaders of Teams

A and B waiting in the woods. Eddie listened to everything, said nothing. He knew Rovan and Wilson were speaking from experience and he agreed with their call on this. It was an incredibly difficult shot. They had only one chance because if Wilson took the shot and missed, the enemy would simply duck completely behind cover and never come back up. They needed to gain more ground and get closer to the enemy.

Below, a squad point man stepped out from the tree line, bravely leading one half of his team toward the outbuildings while the other half remained stationary and gave them cover.

"Smith in the open." Rovan murmured to no one. His glass followed Smith. Everyone felt the tension rising.

Then they heard the blast of sniper fire, and Smith crumpled to the ground even before the shot's echo swept over the hills.

The squad immediately returned fire, and spurts from weapons spilled across the valley. A couple of smoke grenades were flung through the air. The cloud of red fog-covered Smith's body and provided cover to get it back to safety.

Heath watched from the top of the hill, looking blank and undecided.

"We must take him out," Eddie muttered.

"You think I don't know that," Heath said, glaring at Eddie. "Were you not listening to what we discussed just now?"

"I heard everything, but with a dead body, we have no other option. We have to take that shot now or come back with a better plan."

Rovan checked the target's position.

"He's gone," he reported, grimly.

"For now, but he will reappear soon enough. Where he is right now is as fortified as any place could get in this terrain." Eddie said.

"Even if he does, the wind alone makes this a one-in-a-million shot, forget about the distance. What if we don't hit him? We only have one chance. Once he knows he can be hit, he will be gone in an instant, and this time for good," Rovan said.

"I'll take the shot." Eddie was looking at his gun.

"Queer, you are out of your fucking mind," Wilson said.

"Maybe, but I can take this shot. If you still want to do it, I'll wait."

Heath and Rovan looked at Wilson, who was now seething. He didn't like his skills challenged in front of them by a sissy like Eddie.

"Have you forgotten what we did to you last night? If you have, then you might want to check your face." Wilson managed to snigger through his anger.

"You still haven't answered if you can take the shot?" Eddie was calm on the surface. Inside, it was a different story.

If there hadn't been a sniper aiming for their heads, Wilson might have lunged at Eddie for challenging and mocking his skills and authority.

Heath intervened. "You can take it?" he asked Eddie.

"Yes," Eddie said without hesitation.

"What if you miss?" Wilson demanded.

"I'll let Wilson decide that."

"There's going to be a dead body either way," Wilson sniggered. "His or…"

"Right here," Eddie said without missing a beat. His right index finger to his skull, he added, "One-shot."

Rovan and Heath looked at each other with mixed emotions. It was now more than just a mission.

* * *

**Nine minutes before the shot**

The rock was a fucking oven and the wind was strong, blowing from left to right, as Eddie crept up to the vantage point.

Rovan had confirmed Torpedo was visible again.

"You sure you'll hit him?" Rovan asked as Eddie took Wilson's place beside him.

Wilson retreated to take the position beside Heath, both behind the cover of the rocks.

Eddie didn't respond. He looked through the glass at Torpedo. Ninety percent of Torpedo's body was behind the fortified wall; only his head and part of his torso were exposed. He was wearing a green uniform and was holding the Dragunov he'd shot Smith with.

Eddie closed his eyes and his training took over. He got himself quickly but calmly into the perfect sniping position.

Eddie, like every sniper, followed a set pattern, getting the different parts of his body into optimum position in strict order starting with the left hand, followed by the elbows, legs, right hand, and cheek.

Finally, he forced himself to relax and control his breathing, focusing solely on the target.

* * *

**Four minutes before the shot**

The wind's pace rose a notch. Eddie knew all eyes were on him. Rovan, lying beside him, was studying how Eddie was going to take the shot, while Wilson and Heath were ready to pounce on him once he missed.

Eddie understood that sniping, beyond its impossible precision, had an intense psychological impact too; it brought out one's deep-rooted vulnerabilities. One could picture a sniper trying to get a bead on oneself and start making mistakes out of sheer nervousness.

Eddie knew to fire at a soldier was one thing, but trying to find and take out another sniper, especially a highly skilled one like Torpedo, was a whole different ball game.

It was like chess. Both sides knew the game and its rules, making it an even match. He knew winning this battle was more of a mental game than a physical one.

Also, real sniping unlike in movies was different. In the movies, Wahlberg got his target between the crosshairs and squeezed the trigger and that was all it took. In real life, the position of the target that Eddie could see through his scope was not the same as the actual position of the target when his bullet reached him. In the distance of 1300 yards between his rifle's barrel and the target, the earth would shift, gravity would kick in and the wind would play its capricious part. Hitting a still target, even under normal circumstances, was a game of sheer prediction. But the circumstances surrounding this shot required Eddie to foretell the future with precise accuracy.

Eddie had the uncanny ability to mentally record every shot he had ever taken. He remembered the distance, the wind speed, the temperature, the elevation and every damn thing that had played a role in determining his probability of hitting his target. He was a living personification of oneness—he became his gun.

The rifle Eddie was using was the M24 SWS (Sniper Weapon System), the sniper rifle of choice for the United States Army. It was referred to as a "weapon system" because it consisted of not only a rifle but also a detachable telescopic sight and other accessories.

The drawback of Eddie's rifle was that its maximum effective range was 875 yards, although he had recorded shots at over 1050 yards.

So to put it mildly, he was looking to make a first shot count at a target who himself knew all the tricks of the trade and was out of the effective range while hiding in a fortified position that covered 90% of his body. Moreover, Eddie needed to take his enemy out against a strong crosswind that made the trajectory of the bullet almost impossible to guess.

Even if the wind somehow remained steady, everything else being equal, to hit his mark Eddie would have to curve his shot, firing the bullet sixty-five feet away from the target he was aiming at, using the wind velocity and angle of firing to make up for the effective range deficiency. He would use physics to extend the range and power of his gun.

Rovan and Wilson had already considered all these variables and taken into account the margin for error. They were right in concluding that it all added up to 'impossible'.

Any sniper in his right mind wouldn't agree to take such a shot but Eddie's circumstances had made him take up this impossible challenge. If he succeeded, he would silence every last one of his detractors at one go. And if he failed..., well, from the mean look in Wilson's eye, Eddie knew the harassment he'd hitherto faced would probably be the least of his worries.

He lay still, his eyes pushing the glass to the max, his mind in complete control. He had done the calculations thrice in his mind. There was nothing else he could do now.

He finally let off his first and only possible shot, not even remotely pointed toward his target.

Rovan watched the bullet as it moved in a giant banana arc and after what seemed like an eternity, struck Torpedo directly in the face. Rovan saw the red mist in the air and the body of the target falling back behind the fortified wall. No one knew what the coveted target uttered just before he died, but the words that slipped from everyone else who was watching were: "No fucking way."

Eddie closed his eyes and quickly got back behind the safety of the rock. He didn't look at Wilson or Heath, just kept his eyes closed, savoring the moment before it became stale. Although he knew it never would.

* * *

**Four days later**

Sam Wick waited near the temporary open gym space at the base. He had just landed in the country with only one thing to do this time—meet Eddie. He had everything he needed to know about Eddie stashed in his eidetic memory, and now all he had to do was to talk to the man in person.

A certain curiosity had already started building around Wick at the base. That he wasn't a civilian was evident from the way he stood amidst the Delta, Marines and the U.S. Army soldiers. The invisible energy around him told people it would be wise to keep their distance.

At 5'11", Wick's weather-beaten face was ruggedly attractive, not least because of his unreadable sea-blue eyes, bright with intelligence. With his short-cropped black hair and athletic build, he had the appearance of a man on a mission. And he was here on the orders of his bosses at the Task Force–77 (TF–77).

TF–77 was a black ops team jointly created by the NSA and the U.S. Army—an off-the-books team that came into play when diplomatic solutions failed. Powered by NSA intel and U.S. military might across the globe, the team was well-equipped to handle just about anything. It was chosen for the toughest missions in the most dangerous locations using means that no government could officially authorize.

* * *

Eddie was in cuffs when he was brought to Wick. His face and both his eyes were swollen, and he was limping.

Wick watched him closely as he was led across the yard to where he sat.

Was this the guy who had made that impossible shot?

Wick hoped the intel he had been provided was genuine and that he hadn't come here on a wild goose chase.

Eddie stopped at some distance from Wick, confusion writ plain on his face.

"Eddie Vicar?" Wick asked.

Eddie nodded

"Uncuff him," Wick said to the two men who had brought Eddie. The men looked at each other but did nothing.

"He is not a fugitive. Uncuff him now." Wick's tone indicated he wasn't in the mood to repeat himself.

The men hesitated but did as he said. After all, this was an army base and Eddie was in no position to run.

Eddie rubbed his wrists, free of the restraints.

"Five steps back," Wick ordered. The two soldiers looked at each other but obeyed.

Eddie looked at the men backing off and looked back at Wick in surprise.

"Who are you?"

"Sam Wick," Wick said.

Eddie waited for the man to say something more in way of an introduction, but nothing more was forthcoming. *Sam Wick.* Was that all he was going to get from this man?

"Thanks for this," he said, indicating his free hands, trying to fill the awkward silence.

"Why did you volunteer to take that shot?" Wick asked the one question for which he had come to Iraq from Lithuania.

Eddie blinked. Then, he said, "First, who are you? Second, why do you want to know?" It was clear he had difficulty in uttering words.

"I'm the one person standing between your court-martial and freedom. But I don't have all the time in the world to decide if I should bet on you or not. Give me good reasons why I shouldn't leave you rotting in jail."

Eddie studied the man closely. He wasn't a lawyer. Nor was he from Army; maybe he had been once but not anymore. Nor was he some private contractor, otherwise he wouldn't be here, at this base. Special forces, maybe, but Eddie couldn't be sure.

Wick looked at his wristwatch as if he was getting late for something. Was it an act? Eddie couldn't be sure.

"I took that shot because I'm good at math," Eddie responded.

"You think Wilson and Rovan didn't consider everything before backing off from that shot and suggesting that they should gain some ground first?" Wick asked.

"I'm not saying that."

"Then what was different in your calculations?"

"I was the difference."

Wick said nothing. He looked at Eddie, trying to gauge if he was bullshitting him. He wasn't. The man in front of him sincerely believed what he had said.

"In normal circumstances, would you have taken that shot?"

"I don't understand."

"If we were to eliminate your hatred for Wilson and Heath from the equation, would you still have taken that shot?"

"Yes."

"Why?"

"Smith was a good man and a patriot. He shouldn't have died."

"You think Wilson and Heath were responsible for his death?" Wick asked.

"Yes."

"Why are you here, in the U.S. army?"

"Where else should I be?" Eddie tried to smile but winced in pain instead.

"What do you have to say about the U.S. army not supporting you enough despite your skills and services?"

"Nothing."

"Will you still have nothing to say when you're thrown in jail, a very likely scenario as of now?"

Eddie said nothing.

"You shot Wilson and Heath, so when everyone should be hailing you as a hero, you are facing a trial. People are calling you a sicko. I'll be checking if you are medically sound enough, you can bet on that, but tell me, what were you thinking when took those shots?"

"Nothing at the time, but I felt relieved once it was done. As if something that was eating at me from the inside was finally satisfied. If I had wanted to kill them, I would have. But that was never my intention. All I want is that now they'll take my face to their graves. Their scars will keep reminding them."

"I'm sure they would, now that they are bedridden for at least 6 months and their army career is nothing but over. They could have shot back at you."

"I know."

"Insanity or fearlessness?"

"I haven't thought of that moment again, so I can't say what to label it." Eddie was truthful. He had thought of his childhood, during his solitary confinement.

"Who did this to you?" Wick's gaze took in his battered face and body.

"Those who consider Wilson their leader."

"What about Heath? They don't consider him as their commander?"

"He is a dirtbag, a spineless shit. Everyone knows that."

"These men, Wilson's men… they might've killed you too."

"Do I look like I care?"

"Do you believe in God?

"No," Eddie said.

"Why not?"

"Irrelevant."

"This question, or God?"

"Both." Eddie didn't smile this time.

"Angry with Him, or maybe disappointed?" Wick pressed.

"Neither. Just indifferent."

"What do you believe in?"

"In my country."

"Still?"

"Still."

"If you rot in a cell for the rest of your life or die, you are of no use to the country." Wick was slowly homing in on the task he was here for.

Eddie remained silent.

"I am part of a team that works for the government, doing things government doesn't or can't do on their own."

"Offering me a job?"

"Only laying out your options. This one was not on the menu, so I added it," Wick replied.

"Getting out of one shithole and into another one," Eddie smirked.

"One that is less smelly and less assholey."

"Why if I don't like the smell?"

"Haven't met anyone who didn't."

"They left, or died?"

"You choose what suits you best."

"You are not very likable and not at all good at this recruitment thing."

"Not part of my job description," Wick said.

"How much time I have to decide?" Eddie asked.

In response, Wick checked his wristwatch and looked up at Eddie expectedly.

"Now?" Eddie asked dubiously.

Wick looked at him in silence.

"What is this team called?"

"Task Force–77."

"And who are you again?"

"Sam Wick."

Eddie waited again for Wick to say more but in vain.

"I'm in," Eddie said, watching for some change in Wick's expression. He saw nothing, only two blue eyes staring back at him as if trying to determine if Eddie was serious or just eager to get out of his current situation. Then after a pause of ten seconds, Wick got up. "Will be in touch soon."

Eddie nodded not sure of what he should do next. Wick signaled to the two men standing five steps behind, and they herded him back to solitary confinement.

\* \* \*

Driving out of the base in his SUV, Wick reached for his satphone from the bag lying at the passenger seat. He dialed a number from memory. The call was picked up on the second ring and a female voice responded.

"He is in," Wick said.

"Good. We'll take it from here. Angela will be in touch with you about your next mission."

The call was disconnected.

*The End*

\* \* \*

### THE SAM WICK QUADRILOGY: BOOKS 1-4

*Over 700 Pages of Pure adrenaline. Non Stop thrills. Razor-sharp tension. Read the first four thrillers in the best-selling Sam Wick series.*

*"In the tradition of the best thrillers and heroes."*

***His name is Sam Wick.*** *He's the one the U.S. government calls on to extract people out of the worst of the worst enemy places on earth. Where the government cannot and will not go, he will. There is no guarantee that he'll succeed every time but he doesn't have a choice or does he?*

*Fast paced. Hard hitting. Action explodes right off the page. Scroll up to BUY these non-stop thrillers on your devices **NOW!***

**BOOK 1: Wicked Deceit**

*What do you do when your own President wants you dead? You call Sam Wick.*

*His mission: Extract Carlos Cruz-Diez—a New York Times reporter from the clutches of death.*

*Location: Venezuela Consulate in Vienna, Austria.*

*The Obstacle: Venezuela's National Intelligence Service has sent sixteen of their best to execute this mission.*

*Timeline: Twenty-four hours.*

*Time is running out. Bullets are flying. Bodies are piling up. Nothing is as it seems.*

*Will Sam Wick succeed?*

*BOOK 2: Wicked Hunter*

*The Taliban have abducted a CIA agent. No one knows where he is being kept. Time is running out. Can he be saved?*

*His mission: Extract Josh Fletcher, a CIA operative, from the Taliban Backyard*

*Deadline: Less than twelve hours.*

*Can Wick outrun death?*

*BOOK 3: Wicked Blood*

*America is under attack and the world's most powerful nation isn't the least bit ready for it.*

*Can Sam Wick save his motherland?*

*BOOK 4: Wicked Storm*

*A girl's life at stake. A cage match. Only one chance to save her.*

\* \* \*

Get The Box Set Now!

TURN THE PAGE TO READ THE FIRST 2 CHAPTERS OF WICKED DECEIT & DECIDE FOR YOURSELF IF ITS WORTH YOUR TIME.

\* \* \*

# WICKED DECEIT - CHAPTER 1

What could you possibly offer the man who controlled not only your destiny but that of your whole country? The man who ruled with an iron fist. The man who had the Russian President on his speed-dial. The man who had once given the finger to the US President at a diplomatic convention. What could you possibly give the President of your country on his birthday?

But Henrique Arias Cárdenas, the director of the Venezuela Intelligence Service, had more on his mind than a birthday present while he waited in the visitor's lounge of the Palacio de Miraflores—the President of Venezuela's office. He glanced at the 19th-century wall clock above the majestic office door behind which the President was about to meet him. It was thirteen past two in the morning and the city was quiet after a long day of travails, but Henrique wasn't even thinking of sleep. There wasn't any time. He sat at the edge of the couch with his back straight, his hands sweating even in the temperature-controlled room.

Since his phone rang an hour ago, he was racking his brain to construe a reason for the urgency of this meeting but got nothing. Not a pleasant situation to be in, especially for the Director of Venezuela's premier intelligence agency.

He already had a meeting scheduled with the President at eight in the morning, just before the whole country would start celebrating their leader's birthday. Festivities had been planned for the next seven days, and over the past few weeks, he and his men had been busy foiling the attempts by radical extremists to devise disruptions in the celebrations. His office had been diligent in sending daily briefs to the President's office. What then had warranted this late-night summons? What was it that could not wait for six more hours?

One of the officers standing alert near the grand door lifted his right hand to his earpiece and then glanced at Henrique. It was time.

As Henrique fell in step with his escort, he coughed twice, attempting to relax the lump in his throat. It didn't work. He took his hands out of his trouser pockets to reduce the sweating; that didn't work either. Then the big gates opened before him and it was too late to do anything. He took a deep breath and hoped for the best.

．　．　．

The President was standing at the royal desk, his fingers resting on a folded publication. Henrique walked in and stopped at a respectful distance, carefully observing the President's face to gauge his mood. The man was not just upset; he was seething with anger.

He glanced at the publication in the President's hand and recognized the font. It was a copy of the New York Times. He said nothing. The President's laser-focused stare was unsettling, making him unsure of his next steps.

"Venezuela is a mess, a bloody mess." His boss read out the front-page headline, looking straight at him. He jerked his hand, and the newspaper slid across the table to Henrique who stopped it, with a swift gesture, quickly glancing at the columnist's name—Carlos Cruz-Díez. "You know why he can so boldly accuse us of these baseless charges?"

Henrique appeared alarmed by the anger but maintained a stoic silence. It was a rhetorical question.

"I should have killed him. I should have killed him and hanged him for others to see and learn, instead of letting him leave the country."

"We can still do it." Henrique finally had something to offer.

．　．　．

"How?"

"He visited our consulate in Vienna a few days ago."

"Why did no one tell me that?"

"It was in the PDB," Henrique said, referring to the President's daily brief sent by his office.

The President considered it for a moment.

"How soon?"

"He is going to visit again. We can take care of him then if you want."

"How?"

"It's better if you remain unaware of the modalities."

The President weighed this momentarily-Plausible deniability-before a slow smile appeared on his lips. Henrique smiled too. This was his birthday present to the President.

# WICKED DECEIT - CHAPTER 2

Team Vesuvius was already in the briefing room when Sam Wick arrived. The three Vesuvius members - Jessica, Stan, and Mac - looked up as he entered. Their tense postures relaxed slightly at the sight of a familiar face. Wick scanned the space. It was a boardroom kind of setting with a long wide conference table at its center, surrounded by twelve mid-back mesh desk chairs. The wall opposite to the door doubled up as a projector screen. He instinctively walked towards the chair that had clear visibility of both the projector screen and the exit. Sitting down, he observed the others in the room.

Team Vesuvius was one of Task Force 77's (TF-77) support teams. TF-77 was a black ops team jointly created by the NSA and the US Army - an off-the-books team that comes into play when the diplomatic solutions failed. Powered with US military might across the globe and NSA's intel, the team was well equipped to handle anything and that made it the one to go for the toughest missions on the most dangerous locations using means that any government would never authorize yet expect it to get done. During these deadly missions the TF-77's assets, like Sam Wick, were supported by small on-the-ground teams like Vesuvius. These teams typically comprise three to four members—made available to field operatives depending on their mission.

Jessica led the Vesuvius. She was the logistics liaison and an expert in close combat. Stan was a former marine and an Olympic-level shooter. Mac was the go-to guy for anything remotely associated with technology. Together these three represented one of TF-77's ace support teams.

Wick knew of the Vesuvius team and each one of its members. Though nothing in his expression showed it, he was glad he would be going into this mission with them.

**Get the Boxset Now!**
**Sam Wick Rapid Thrillers**

**\* \* \***

# YOUR FREE BOOK

**Do not forget to download your FREE COPY of WICKED STORM.**

**Check - www.thechaseaustin.com**

## DEDICATION

To My Readers

# ACKNOWLEDGEMENT

Special thanks to my **advance readers group** who are nothing but supportive of my writing and extremely helpful in rectifying mistakes that could have ruined the experience of reading this story.

.

# ABOUT THE AUTHOR

**_Dear Fabulous Reader,_**

_Thank you for reading. If you're a fan of Sam Wick, spread the word to friends, family, book clubs, and reader groups online. I would love to hear from you. Let's connect @_
_www.thechaseaustin.com_
_chaseaustincreative@gmail.com_
_Join my Facebook group below to get behind the scene content or follow me on Goodreads, Instagram or BookBub._

Printed in Great Britain
by Amazon